Resounding praise for
the incomparable western fiction of
New York Times bestselling Grand Master

ELMORE LEONARD

"Leonard began his career telling western stories. He knows his way onto a horse and out of a gun fight as well as he knows the special King's English spoken by his patented, not-so-lovable urban lowlifes."

Milwaukee Journal Sentinel

"In cowboy writing, Leonard belongs in the same A-list shelf as Louis L'Amour, Owen Wister, and Zane Grey."

New York Daily News

"Leonard wrote westerns, very good westerns . . . the way he imagined Hemingway, his mentor, might write westerns."

Baton Rouge Sunday Advocate

"A master . . . Etching a harsh, haunting landscape with razor-sharp prose, Leonard shows in [his] brilliant stories why he has become the American poet laureate of the desperate and the bold . . . In stories that burn with passion, treachery, and heroism, the frontier comes vividly, magnificently to life."

Tulsa World

"[Leonard's stories] transcend the genre to work as well as any serious fiction of the era—or

Books by Elmore Leonard

ELMORE LEONARD

Three-Ten to Yuma
and other stories

HarperTorch
An Imprint of HarperCollinsPublishers

This is a work of fiction. The characters, incidents, and dialogue are drawn from the author's imagination and are not to be construed as real. Any resemblance to actual events or persons, living or dead, is entirely coincidental.

♦

HARPERTORCH
An Imprint of HarperCollins*Publishers*
10 East 53rd Street
New York, New York 10022-5299

Copyright © 2006 by Elmore Leonard, Inc.
The Complete Western Stories of Elmore Leonard copyright © 2004 by Elmore Leonard, Inc.
Map designed by Jane S. Kim
Collection editor, Gregg Sutter
ISBN-13: 978-0-06-112164-7
ISBN-10: 0-06-112164-9

First HarperTorch paperback printing: December 2006

The stories contained in this volume appeared in *The Complete Western Stories of Elmore Leonard*, published in December 2004 by William Morrow, an imprint of HarperCollins Publishers.

HarperCollins®, HarperTorch™, and ♦™ are trademarks of HarperCollins Publishers Inc.

Printed in the United States of America

Visit HarperTorch on the World Wide Web at www.harpercollins.com

10 9 8 7 6 5 4 3 2 1

☆ Contents ☆

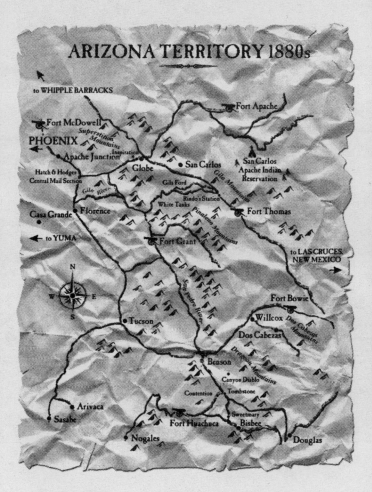

Three-Ten to Yuma
and other stories

1

Cavalry Boots

ON THE MORNING of May the tenth, 1870, four troops of cavalry, out of Fort Bowie and at full strength, met a hundred-odd Mimbreño Apaches under Chee about a mile east of what used to be Helena. Cavalry met Apache on open, flat terrain—which happened seldom enough—and they cut the Indians to ribbons. Only Chee and a handful of his warriors escaped.

On the official record the engagement is listed as the Battle of Dos Cabezas. But strictly speaking the title is misleading, for the twin peaks of Dos Cabezas were only a landmark to the south. The engagement broke the back of an Apache uprising, but that is not the important point. The Reservation at San Carlos is mute testimony that all uprisings did fail.

No, the importance of the Dos Cabezas action is in how it happened to come about; and the record is not complete on that score—though there is a statement in the record meant to explain how cavalry was able to meet guerrilla Apache away from his mountain stronghold. And there is mention of the unnatural glow in the night sky that attracted both cavalry and Apache. But still, the record is incomplete.

Stoneman himself, Brigadier General, Department of Arizona, was at Bowie at the time. That is why much of the credit for the engagement's success is given to him. However, the next week at Camp Grant, Stoneman made awards connected with the action. The Third United States Dragoons received a unit citation. A Lieutenant R. A. Gander was cited for bravery; it being consolation for a shattered left leg. One other award was made. And therein lies the strange story of the Dos Cabezas affair.

This is how it happened.

* * *

ALWAYS, IT IS preceded by quiet.

The silence creeps over the gray gloom that is the

desert at night and even the natural night sounds are not there. Off, far off, against the blackness of a mountainside there appears the orange-red smear of a bonfire. From a distance it is a flickering point of light, cold and alone. And then—

THE APACHES ARE UP!

It is a scream down the length of the barracks adobe.

Through the window, Kujava sees the thin slash of red in the blackness to the east and he pulls his boots on mechanically, grimly.

Then he is First Sergeant Kujava, swinging through the barracks with a booming voice and a leather gauntlet slashing at sleeping feet. Kujava knows men. He asks them if they want to be late to die and he does it with a roar of a laugh so they cannot refuse. With the recruits, it is effective. They leap up and yell and laugh with an eagerness that means they are new to frontier station.

And it shows they do not know the Apache.

Others remain motionless, but with eyes open, seeing the desert and the dust-covered mesquite and the alkali and the screaming whiteness of the sun all combined in a shimmering, oppressing haze that sears the eyeballs of a white man until a knot tightens around his forehead. That, and salt sweat and the gagging nitrogen smell of the animals beneath them. Stillness, and never an Apache in sight. These are the ones who have been in as long as Kujava.

On Bud Nagle, the dawn rousing had a bewildering effect. He sat bolt upright on his cot and saw the first sergeant running down the narrow aisle, but what the sergeant was calling made no sense to him. He frowned and rubbed his eyes at the commotion, then fell back slowly on his cot and remained motionless. But he did not see the desert. There was a cobblestone street with store fronts and restaurants, and it was east of the Mississippi.

By the end of his first month Bud Nagle had known he was not a cavalryman. He knew he was not a soldier of any kind, but after seven months, it was too late to do anything about it, and even the office door in Milwaukee that bore the legend *L. V. Nagle, Attorney,* could not prevail against it. Enlistments do not dissolve, even if the recruit realizes he is out of place; and especially were they not dissolving that spring of 1870 when Apacheria, from the Dragoons to the San Andres, was vibrating with the beat of hundreds of war drums. The Apaches were up and Cochise would not be stopped.

Now he saw the street again. The shouting, laughing people and the ordinarily shy girls who giggled and threw their arms around the returning soldiers and kissed them right on the street. Right on Wisconsin Avenue. He remembered the deep-blue uniforms and the glistening boots and the one-eyed angle of the kepis, and he could hardly wait.

The uniforms disappeared from the cobblestone street. They had been gone for almost five years, but never from the mind of Bud Nagle. Smiling girls and glistening boots.

By the time he found out how long issue boots kept a shine, it was too late. He was in Apache country.

Now he opened his eyes and looked full into the awe-inspiring face of the first sergeant. Deep-brown hollow cheeks and full cavalry mustache.

"Get off that bunk 'fore I kick your comfort-lovin' butt across the parade!" And he was off down the aisle.

It was always the same. Kujava pulled him from his cot, drilled him until his legs shook with weakness. The corporal swore and gave him extra duty, full pack, four hours on the parade. He was always the handiest when their ire was up and he never learned to keep his mouth shut. The fact that nothing he did was ever done in a military fashion made it doubly easy for the noncoms, and the contagion of their bullying even spread to the ranks.

He was easy to insult and seemed even to invite it. He was not a soldier among soldiers. He tried to act like a man without looking like one. And he complained. That's part of Army life: a big part.

But he whined when he should have bitched like a man. Soldiers know soldiers. They didn't know Bud Nagle.

After only three weeks at Camp Grant he found himself alone. From habit, he continued a pathetic campaign to join the ranks, but at night, in the darkness of the barracks, when in the quietness he could think, Bud Nagle understood that he hated the Army and the men in it. He hated both to the depths of his soul.

✯ ✯ ✯

BY MIDAFTERNOON B Troop was almost thirty miles south of Camp Grant. To the southwest were the Dragoons, and to the east, the Chiricahuas, looming hazy but ominous in the distance. Somewhere up in the towering rocks was the stronghold of Cochise. This wide semi-desert corridor was the gateway to Sonora. Through it passed the Apache raiders into Mexico. Stoneman's Department of Arizona was shaking off its winter lethargy by sending patrols to every corner of the frontier.

Lieutenant R. A. Gander, riding at the head of B Troop, waited until the twin peaks of Dos Cabezas faced him from an eleven o'clock angle, less than a mile to the south, then he rested the patrol for an hour before turning east. B Troop was at the south end of its patrol. It would swing eastward for a few miles, then swing again slightly north and bivouac near Fort Bowie at the mouth of Apache Pass. From there, the last leg was the thirty miles back to Grant.

Soon they were in the foothills of the Chiricahuas. The mountains rose high above them to the south, and on all sides now were timbered hills and massive rock formations through which the trail twisted and climbed, seldom in sight ahead for more than a hundred yards.

It was dangerous country to take a patrol through. Gander knew that, but sometimes you had to offer a little bait in the business of fighting Indians. That, and the fact that a young officer tends to become careless after too many months of garrison duty. He becomes eager. Gander had not seen an Apache in six months.

He rode with the self assurance that he was a natural leader. They don't give commissions to everyone. He was following patrol instructions to the letter, a routine laid down by a much higher authority than his own, and Lieutenant Gander had complete faith in his superiors. At the Point that had become as natural to him as walking.

He had sent point riders ahead to safeguard against ambush, with explicit orders to make frequent contact.

No danger of being cut off. It was strict military

procedure, always on the alert. It was patrol precaution, outlined and detailed in the Manual. So Gander was confident.

Unfortunately, Chee had not read the Manual. Nor had any of his Mimbreño Apaches.

Chee knew everything he needed to know about Lieutenant Gander and his forty-man patrol. He had known it before the troop was five miles south of Grant. The size of the patrol, their equipment, and their experience. In the endless expanse of Arizona sky there were thin wisps of smoke and sudden flashes of the sun's reflection caught on polished metal. That morning the signals had been many and Chee moved over a hundred warriors from the *rancheria* high up in the Chiricahuas to the foothills.

He scattered them along both sides of the trail where the irregular road suddenly opened up and sloped into a flat, broad area almost a mile long and three hundred yards wide. He hid his warriors behind rock and scrub brush hours before the patrol reached Dos Cabezas and swung eastward into the foothills. And he laid his ambush with contempt for the soldier who was fool enough to establish a pattern of operation in enemy territory.

Chee made no sign when Gander's point riders came into view from the narrow, sloping trail. His face was unlined and impassive, but in the calmness

of his dark face there was an eye-squinting stern-
ness that told of other things. It told of his father,
Mangas Coloradas, who had been shot in the back
as he lay on the ground tied hand and foot. Trussed
up and shot from behind after he had accepted a
white flag.

✯ ✯ ✯

SERGEANT KUJAVA, leading point, sent a rider out to
the extremities on both sides of the open space. He
rode in silence, his head swiveling from one side to
the other, taking in every rock and tree clump, his
eyes climbing the steel walls of brush and rock that
revolted against the sandy flatness to rise abruptly on
both sides and finally stretch into rolling foothills.
He paid no attention to Bud Nagle riding at his side.
He had stopped lecturing him at Dos Cabezas.

He walked his mount slowly, and every so often
he stood up in the stirrups and gazed straight
ahead. And in the alert mind of First Sergeant Kujava there was an uneasiness. He didn't like the
stillness.

Bud Nagle wiped the palm of his hand across his
mouth and then pulled his hat brim closer to his
eyes while his tongue felt along the dryness that
crusted his lips. He swore feebly against the country
and made his mind to go far away where there was
greenness and a cool breeze and streetcar tracks.

His dull eyes fell to his uniform shirt that was fading from the saturation of body salt. His head rolled to the side and he looked at boots that could be any color under the crust of white dust.

At the north end of the pocket, where rock and brush squeezed in again to resume its rugged stinginess, the narrowness brought the two outriders in to join the sergeant and Nagle. Ahead, the trail sloped gradually through a rock pass and then broadened into a timber-flanked aisle that stretched into the distance and finally ended in a yellowness that was the plain.

Kujava held the riders up and turned in his saddle to see the patrol just entering the open area.

"Stretch your legs," he told them. "They're too far behind. That's how you get cut off."

The two outriders dismounted and led their mounts to the side of the trail where a clump of pines cast a triangle of shade. They sat on the ground and stretched stiff legs out in front of them.

Kujava turned his horse around. He slouched in the saddle, one leg hooked over the saddle horn, and watched the hazy line of blue approaching in the distance. He watched the patrol reach the midpoint of the pocket, and the unnatural silence gnawed at his brain and made the ring seem sharper in his ears. He swung his boot back to the stirrup, uneasy, wanting to be ready, and as he did so he heard the *click*.

Not wood, like a twig snapping. It was metal grinding against metal, and it was sharp and clear enough to send the flash of honest fear through his body and jerk him to the reaction of a man who knows combat. He yanked rein to drag his mount about sharply and tugged his carbine from its boot in the motion, for a Spencer will make that very click when the breech is opened, and the click is loud if the piece is rusted—rusted and uncared for, like the carbine an Apache would have!

He shouted and swung up the carbine, but the shout was drowned in a crash of gunfire and the motion was lost in the phantasm of a hundred impressions as the basin exploded its ambush and caught B Troop by the throat.

Kujava shouted and fired and shouted, and he saw his outriders sprawled in their triangle of shade. And he saw Bud Nagle still sitting his horse with both hands frozen to the saddle horn, his back a ramrod and his eyes popped open in white circles of fear and disbelief.

"Nagle, ride! Ride!" Kujava's arm swung as he screamed at the stiff-bodied trooper and struck him across the shoulder.

"Get out of here—ride like hell to Bowie—before they're on to us!"

Nagle moved and seemed to be suddenly drenched with the excitement so that it washed through him and took with it his nerve and his reason.

And the simplicity of Bud Nagle said, "I don't know where it is."

Strange things happen in combat. Kujava's jaw dropped and he wanted to laugh, even with the firing—because of the firing, but it was only for an instant.

He swung his carbine against the rump of Nagle's mount, sending it into a jolting start down the narrow trail.

"Ride, dammit! Ride!"

His hands were frozen to the saddle horn, his eyes still wide open, seeing nothing, as his mount broke through the rocky narrowness in a gallop, sliding almost sideways in the loose gravel, careening from one rock wall to the other until hoofs struck firm ground at the bottom and raced on, momentum up, along the timber-lined aisle.

He strained his eyes against the distance as if this would draw the safety of it closer to him; as if he would be shielded from the pressing blackness of the heavy timber by holding his neck rigid to look only straight ahead. In a way it was a comfort, but because of it he didn't see the four ponies come out of the timber behind him. Four ponies painted for war and carrying Mimbreño Apaches.

He reached the end of the aisle and swung out onto the open plain, riding into the vastness, unsure of the direction, kicking his mount frantically toward the low horizon. Hoofs pounded packed sand and the sound vibrated against his mind to keep the knot tight inside of him, taking the place of the excitement of combat that was now a faint rattle far behind.

In his fear he was unmindful of time, his eyes straining against the distance. Then, in the haze, the horizon changed.

A dark line interrupted the monotonous tone of the plains, stretching and taking shape. It came closer yard by yard and finally there it was. A town. A real town!

He was a mile or more away when the shot rapped from behind. He turned to see the Apaches less than two hundred yards behind, then kicked hard and angled for the frame structures in the distance.

The Mimbres closed the gap by another two dozen yards before Bud Nagle reached the edge of the town, and as he wheeled to head into the street, a second shot slapped against the wide openness like a barrel stave against concrete, and horse and rider went down.

Bud Nagle was stunned. He sat in the dust shaking his head while the dust and his mind cleared.

He wanted to rest, but the rumble of the ponies behind him jerked him stumbling to his feet. He tried to run before he was all the way up and he fell to his hands and knees, crawled, then rose to his feet again and ran a few yards yelling at the top of his voice before he stumbled again, sprawling full length in the thick dust of the road.

The dust filled his open mouth and choked his screams for help, muffling the words to make them incoherent and all the more pitiful. He screamed and choked and drove his legs so savagely that he fell again as he reached the three steps to a porch, hitting his knees against the steps repeatedly until he climbed to the porch and lunged through the swing-type doors of the building.

He stopped in the gloom of the interior, throwing out his arms to rest against a support post in the middle of the room. His body sagged with relief as he put his head against the post, trying to catch his breath.

A hoarseness came out of his throat forming the words, "Apaches—Apaches! Right outside town!"

The silence answered him. And it was so loud and mocking that the breath caught in his throat.

He lifted his head slowly because he knew what he would see and he didn't want to see it. Finally he straightened his head and looked at the dust that couldn't be less than a dozen years old. It covered every surface of the bare room.

He made his head swing along an arc, taking in the rectangular strip of lighter-colored flooring where the bar had stood, and on toward the front of the room. His body moved and a boot scraped the gritty floor.

His shoulders jerked upward and his whole body tensed in an unnatural rigid position. His gaze sank into a dingy front corner and he kept his eyes on the shadowed line where wall met wall, as if by seeing nothing, nothing would see him. Slowly, neck muscles relaxed and the line of his jaw eased. He turned his eyes to the doorway.

A patch of dirty gray light showed through the opening above the louvered doors. Below, a square of the front porch stood out vividly, framed by the blackness of the doors and the dismal gloom of the inside of the room. The doors hung silently against the evening light, rickety and fragile because of the louvers, forming a thin, flimsy barrier against the outside.

He knew he was alone in a one-block town—alone with four Apaches.

And the desolate, stone-silent town squeezed in through the darkening gloom with a ring to its silence that was overbearing, and it pushed the thin figure back into the shadows.

The uniform hung loose and empty-looking as he backed away, lifting his feet gently, holding his arms close to his sides. His right arm brushed the holster on his hip and he glanced down and up quickly as if afraid to take his eyes from the doorway. But his drawn face relaxed slightly as he fumbled at the holster and drew the long-barreled revolving pistol.

Suddenly he stopped. A sharpness jolted against his spine, and he wheeled, discharging the heavy pistol wildly. He fired four times, running, stumbling toward the stairway along the back wall. The explosions slammed against the empty room, bouncing from wall to wall in an ear-splitting din, and with it was the sharp clattering of broken glass. He raced up the stairs, leaving the barroom alone, bare but for the center post against which he had bumped.

And again the silence.

In the upstairs room he pressed stiff-backed to the wall just inside the door while his chest heaved and his head jerked in spasms from the door to the front windows that were dim gray squares outlining the evening. Slowly he edged along the wall until he reached a corner window and pressed his cheek to the frame.

From the angle he could see almost the entire length of the block-long town. Adobe and clapboard squatted side by side, gaunt and ugly and with a flimsy coldness that proclaimed their unoccupancy. Ramadas extended from most of the building fronts, rickety and drooping, pushing out into the street to squeeze the dirt road into a rutted narrowness. The ramadas hid most of the lower windows and doorways that lined the street, casting a deeper shadow in the fast-falling gloom.

Then, from somewhere below, there was creak of a board bending on a rusted nail. He froze to the wall and the sound stopped.

It tightened every nerve and muscle in his body; but he moved his legs, his hand shaking with the weight of the revolving pistol. He made his way across the room to the door and looked out to the dim landing, leaning over the railing and listened, but only the ragged cut of his breath interrupted the stillness. He backed from the stairway along the short hall that ended a few feet behind him.

A glass-paned door opened to an outside landing with a decaying stairway falling steeply to the ground. The last of the evening light seeped into the narrowness between the two buildings and lost most of its strength filtering through the grimy panes of the door glass. He glanced over his shoulder through one of the panes seeing only the landing and the rotting board wall of the next building, which was a livery stable.

He approached the blackness of the stairwell again, and as he leaned forward the muffled sound came from below. It was faint, faraway, like leather on wood, but it rasped against his spine like an off-chord and he felt his neck hairs bristle.

He stood rigid, working his mouth to scream, but the scream came out a moan, and the moan a sob, and he kept saying, "Please God—please God—please God—" until he finally turned, slamming into the door, smashing his pistol through the glass panes when the door would not open at once, kicking boots and knees against the door panel.

Then he was out and down the stairs, stopping a moment in the narrow alley to swing his head both ways. An instant later he disappeared through the side door of the next building.

In the upper hall a vague shadow emerged from the blackness of the stairwell to the landing where Bud Nagle had stood. The figure was obscure, but the last of the evening's faint light showed dimly on the head of the Mimbreño war lance.

★ ★ ★

A MIMBREÑO APACHE is not a fanatic. He will not throw his life away. If mortally wounded, the chances are he will put aside precaution to make his last act that of killing a white man. Many white men will do the same. It is not fanaticism; it is complete resignation. Fatalism with fate staring you in the face.

A Mimbre is a little man, less than five-seven, but

he is an oiled-leather cord with rock-tight knots all the way down. He wears a calico band to hold back shoulder-length hair, and his moccasins reach the midpoint of his thighs. He wears a cotton breech-clout and his upper body is painted vermilion. Paint on dirt.

His God is U-sen, and he is the best natural guerrilla fighter in the world. He is a strategist. He lives to kill—and he plans it every hour he's awake while he drinks tizwin to make sure the kill-urge will not go away. And don't you forget it: *He does not throw his life away.*

That is why the three shadows converged on the stable, but without a war cry, without assault. There was not even the hint of noise. The shadows were unreal, blending with the gloom. They moved to the side of the building to join the fourth shadow standing in the narrow alley. The phantom shapes fused together to become a part of the deeper shadow close to the side of the stable.

In a few minutes the obscure figures reappeared, moving quickly, taking definite shape upon reaching the street, then fading again, passing under the ramadas on the other side. And in the narrow alley there was a flicker of light. A wavering, dancing speck of light. Then, vivid orange against black as the fire gradually climbed the decaying wall of the stable.

It was a matter of only a few minutes. The fire scaled the side wall slowly at first; small orange tongues, scattered along the dry surface, finally ate into each other and erupted into a brilliant mass of flame.

For the figure crouched inside the stable there was no choice. He edged out of a stall and moved toward the front of the stable, watching the fire, fascinated, until the flames reached the loft above him and the heat pressed close and smothering.

For a few minutes he forgot about the Apaches, his mind coping with just one thing at a time, and not relating the fire to the Indians. He was completely fascinated, moving toward the front slowly, reluctant to take his eyes from the dancing flames, until the heat licked close and he turned to find himself at the front entrance.

Hiding was out of the question. Swept out by the fire and the panic that strapped his mind and made his heart hammer against his chest.

Panic and no choice.

It made him throw his shoulder against the heavy swing door and force his body through the narrow opening. He hesitated a long second, then ran to the left, hitting the duckboard sidewalk in four strides, then up the steps of the barroom porch. He hesitated again in the deep shadows of the ramada, glanced back toward the stable grinding his teeth together to keep from crying out, then ran across the porch.

At the end of the porch he glanced back again, and that was his mistake.

He turned to break into a run, but the stairs were there and he pitched forward, throwing his arms out in front of him. There was the half-scream and the explosion and that was all. He lay faceup. A thin hole in his chest showed where he had shot himself. And the toes of his issue boots pointed to the red glow that was spreading in the sky.

★ ★ ★

IT WAS THE same glow that brought Apache and cavalry to meet the next morning on the flat plain east of the town of Helena.

Cause and effect is natural. Cavalry followed the glow in the night sky for an obvious reason. That was why there was a garrison at Fort Bowie. Chee brought his Mimbres through a mistake in judgment. Fire in the sky to the northeast, the direction of Fort Bowie. And Cochise, with over two hundred Chiricahuas, was on the warpath in that general direction. It was easy for Chee to abandon one ambushed troop for a chance to assist in the sack of a whole garrison.

An error in judgment and overeagerness. And

when Chee discovered his error it was too late. He was in the open. One of Stoneman's scouts learned this from a Mimbre who survived the battle. The story influenced Stoneman's reasoning. There is no question of that.

That afternoon they found Bud Nagle. His gun empty and his body mutilated. The right hand and foot hacked off. There was only one conclusion to be reached.

At Camp Grant the next week, Stoneman awarded him posthumously the medal that bears Minerva's head. The Medal of Honor.

Regimental pride is a strange thing. A soldier will cling to it because it is important, and he will even let it bias his mind. West of the San Andres there was little else but regimental pride.

Stoneman gave Nagle the Medal of Honor because he had sacrificed his life for his troop. He had fired the town to signal the Bowie garrison, thereby giving his own life. Stoneman even hinted that Nagle signaled with the intention of luring Chee. He did not state it flatly, but moved around it with tactical terms.

That's what regimental pride will do. A hero. His name listed forever on the Roll of Honor of B Troop, Third United States Dragoons. And many believed it—even knowing Bud Nagle— Yes, that's what regimental pride will do.

2

Under the Friar's Ledge

STRUGGLES' ATTITUDE TOWARD the Sangre del Santo story was one of complete indifference. At the time he first heard the story, he was contract surgeon at Fort Huachuca with no time for chasing lost mine legends. It was common knowledge that Struggles had more than a superficial interest in precious metals—it was evident in the way he wangled assignments to extended patrols and would have his pan out at every water stop, and the leaves on which he went into the Dragoons alone with a pack mule and a shovel—but prospecting, to Struggles, was a world apart from chasing legends. Lost mines were for fools, or anyone too lazy to swing a pick and build a sluice box. Listening to the tale, Struggles' rough-grained campaigner's face would wrinkle like soft leather and a half smile would frame the cigar that was clamped between his teeth.

But that was while he was still at Huachuca. That was before he met Juan Solo.

In Soyopa, which is in the state of Sonora, there was another story related along with the one of Sangre del Santo. It concerned Juan Solo who made his home in Soyopa, and very simply, it told that Juan Solo, the Indian-Mexican, knew the exact location of the lost mine. And once a year, they said, he would bring to the tienda a half bar of solid silver weighing one thousand ounces, a weight not used since the departure of the Spanish. And the storekeeper, who was becoming very rich, would allow Juan to purchase whatever he pleased for the rest of the year.

When questioned about the mine, Juan Solo would smile, just as Doctor Struggles was doing at that very time up at Fort Huachuca, and he would shake his head and walk away.

They said that Juan Solo was one of Gokliya's Apaches until Gokliya turned wild and the Mexicans began calling him *Hieronymo*. They said Juan was lazy by nature and became tired of running, so he left the band and became Mexican. But changing his nationality did not erase from his memory the mine he had discovered hiding out in the Sierra Madre with Gokliya. And finally, after the Apache war chief was packed off to Florida, Juan Solo was free to visit his secret mine.

They said he could have been the richest man in Mexico, but his only concern was for mescal and a full bean pot to answer the growl in his belly. Spending any more would have been wasteful. On one occasion, two men resentful of Juan's niggardly attitude followed him into the range when he left for his annual collection. One came back a month later—with his mind still in the hills. The other never returned. It was a long time before anyone tried it again . . . but that was when Struggles entered the story. . . .

In 1638, the Sangre del Santo was mining more silver than any diggings in New Spain with free, Indian labor. But perhaps the Spanish overseers and their protecting garrison were somewhat more demanding than was ordinarily common. The story has it that a Franciscan friar, Tomas Maria, could stand the inhuman treatment of the Tarahumare laborers no longer and so caused them to revolt.

It is said the Spanish killed Tomas Maria for putting thoughts into the heads of the Tarahumares; and after the uprising, in which the Spanish were taken by surprise and annihilated, the Indians found the padre's body and laid it away inside the entrance to the mine. Then they sealed it and defaced the mountainside so there would be no trace of the entrance. The adobe quarters of the Spanish were caved in and spread about until they again became part of the land. The country was restored, and the legend of Tomas Maria's spirit protecting the mine was handed down from father to son.

In Soyopa, the villagers crossed themselves when the name Tomas Maria was mentioned. Then someone would smile and say that the padre and Juan Solo must indeed be good friends, and then everyone would smile. . . .

On a morning in early summer, Juan Solo left Soyopa prodding his burro unhurriedly in the direction that pointed toward the wild, climbing Sierra Madre.

A month before, Struggles had entered Sonora and started down the Bavispe. It had taken a long time to shake soldiering out of his life.

He had been contract surgeon all through most of the campaigns, from before Apache Pass to Crook's border expedition, and in those days he was too busy doctoring to give in completely to the urge that had been growing since his first year in the Southwest. Sometimes the troopers kidded him about it and accused him of knowing every rock within a five mile radius of Thomas, Bowie and Fort Huachuca. Struggles took it with a smile because there was little enough to laugh about at that time.

He wasn't a fanatic about gold. Some men eat and breathe it and know nothing else. Struggles simply thought prospecting was a good idea. Sun and fresh air, hard work, enough excitement to keep your blood circulating regularly and the chance of becoming rich for life. Finally, after almost twenty years of campaigning, he reasoned that his obligation to the Army was at an end. He had served long enough that no one could say he had signed up just for the free transportation.

He worked the Dragoons for almost a year with only a few pyrite showings and then a trace that would die out before it had hardly started. It was enough discouragement to make him look for a new field. He decided to point south and follow the Bavispe down through Sonora, keeping the Sierra Madre on his left, working the foothills until he had the feel of the country, then go deeper into the range.

Five days after Juan Solo left his pueblo, Struggles found him in a barranca. They did not speak, because Juan was unable to. He was spread on his back in the middle of the depression, stripped, his hands and feet fastened with rawhide and pegged deep into the sand. Near him were the ashes of a fire over which his feet had been held before he was staked to the ground.

They spoke of it for a long time after in Soyopa. How Juan Solo rode out one morning on his burro and returned a week later tied to the animal with the American leading it, along with his own, and how the American stayed on with Juan at his adobe and tended him until his sickness passed.

★ ★ ★

STRUGGLES DID NOT consider saving Juan's life a special act of charity. He would have done the same for anyone. Nor did the man's reluctance to explain completely what had occurred bother Struggles. At first, all Juan offered in explanation was that an American, a man whom he had trusted as a friend, caught him unaware and performed this torture on him. Struggles accepted this without pressing conversation and gradually, as his wounds healed, Juan Solo became more at ease. A natural friendship was developing, in spite of their extremely opposite backgrounds.

Finally, one day when Juan's burns were almost healed, he said to Struggles: "That was a good thing you did before." It was his way of thanking Struggles for saving his life.

The surgeon brushed it off. "No more than any man would have done," he said.

Juan Solo frowned. "It is not of such a simple nature. There was a good thing you did before."

Struggles waited while Juan Solo unhurriedly formed the words in his mind.

"Once," Juan began, "I had a friend who desired to be rich. He begged me to show him silver, so I took him into the hills. But even being a friend, I blindfolded his eyes lest avarice lead him back for more, though I meant to give him plenty enough. For two days I walked behind his burro picking up the kernels of maize that he was dropping to mark the trail. And at the end of that time, I unbound his eyes and returned to him all the maize he had dropped, saying such a wasteful man would indeed not know how to use silver. And there I left him, discovering that he was no friend.

"The next time I went out from the pueblo, he was waiting for me and he took me and demanded that I show him the place of the silver. He had Mexican men with him, and at his word they built a fire to abuse the truth from me, as if the words would come from my feet; but I would not speak, so they left me to die."

Juan Solo's eyes did not leave Struggles' hard-lined face. He went on, "Now I have learned that friendship is not simply of words. Man, I will show you silver; as much as your burro can carry will be yours. And there will be no blindfold."

Struggles cleared his throat and felt a flush of embarrassment. "Juan, I didn't treat you for a fee." And then was sorry he had said it when the Indian's sleepy eyes opened suddenly.

But his voice remained even when he said, "To a friend, you offer a gift. You do not repay him." He hesitated. "And I say *offer,* for you need not accept it. Approaching El Sangre del Santo is not the same as entering the great city of Chihuahua. Often there is danger."

Struggles' cigar almost slipped from his mouth. "You know where it is?" he asked, amazed.

The Indian nodded his head.

Sketchily then, the story of the mine formed in the surgeon's head. He relaxed in his chair, putting the pieces together. He had almost forgotten the legend of Tomas Maria.

"What about the padre who acts as watchman?" he asked cautiously. "Is he the danger you spoke of?"

Juan Solo smiled faintly. "Here they say that he and I are good friends. No, the danger is from those who would take all the wealth from the poor padre."

Struggles smiled at the Indian and said, "I imagine he gets pretty lonely up there," but Juan Solo only shrugged his shoulders. Struggles added, "I mean your ex-friend, the American."

The Indian nodded. "After leaving me the thought would come to him that if I died his chance of discovering the mine would be remote. So he would return and find that someone had taken me. First he would curse, then inquire discreetly through one of his men if I had been brought to Soyopa; and finding this to be so, his choice would then be to wait for me to go out again and then to follow."

"Well, you're just guessing now," Struggles said.

Juan Solo shrugged again. "Perhaps."

On the fourth day after leaving the pueblo, Juan's conjecture came back to Struggles suddenly. From that afternoon on, there was little room in his mind for doubting the Indian's word.

They were in high, timbered country moving their horses and pack mules single file along a trail that cut into the pines, climbing to distant rimrock. Where the slope leveled, they came out onto a bench that opened up for a dozen yards revealing, down over the tops of the lower pines and dwarf oaks, the country they had left hours before. In the timber it was cool; but below, the sandy flats and the scattered rock eruptions were all the same glaring yellow, hazy through a dust that hung motionless. At first, Struggles thought he was seeing sun spots from the glare.

He blinked before squinting again and now he was certain there were no sun spots. Far off against the yellow glare, a confused number of moving specks were pointing toward the deep shadows of a barranca. Juan Solo was watching with the palm of his hand shading his eyes.

He looked at the surgeon when the specks passed out of sight. "Now there is no doubt," he said.

Struggles' rough face turned to him quickly. "Why, that could be anybody."

"Señor Doctor," Juan said quietly. "This is my country."

★ ★ ★

AT SUNDOWN they stopped long enough to eat a cold supper, then moved on into a fast-falling gloom. The country was level now, but thick with brush; mesquite clumps which in the evening dimness clung ghostlike to the ground and were dead silent with no breeze to stir them. Struggles, riding behind the Indian, felt his eyes stretched open unnaturally and told himself to quit being a damn fool and relax.

He chewed on the end of the dead cigar and let his stomach muscles go loose, but still a tension gripped him which his own steadying words could not detach. They were being followed. He knew that now, and didn't have to close his eyes to picture what would happen if they were overtaken. But there was more to the feeling than that. It was also the country—the climbing, stretching, never-ending wildness of the country. The Sierra Madre was like the sea, he thought. Both of them deathless, monotonously eternal, and so indifferent in their magnitude that either could accept the dust of all the world's dead and not have the decency to show it in posture. He thought: *Now I know what people mean about wanting to die in bed.* But again he told himself to shut up, because it was foolish to talk.

There was only a soft squeak of saddle leather and the muffled clop of hoofs on sand, and ahead, the dim figure of Juan Solo moving silently, rhythmically to the sounds.

The dusk thickened into night, and later Struggles could feel the ground beneath him changing though he could make out nothing in the darkness. There was a closeness above him along with the more broken ground, so that he sensed rather than observed that they were passing into rockier country.

And when first morning light reflected in the sky, Struggles saw that they were deep into a canyon. Ahead, it twisted out of sight, but beyond the rim a wall of mountain rose a thousand feet into the sky, tapering into a slender pinnacle at one end of its unbalanced crest. It seemed close enough to hit with a stone, but it was at least two miles beyond the canyon.

Juan Solo reined in gently and raised his arm toward the peak, pointing a finger. "Señor Doctor," he said. "Be the first American to observe El Sangre del Santo . . . and know it."

Struggles was unprepared. "That's it?" he said incredulously; then wondered why he had expected it to appear differently. Lost mines needn't look like lost mines. Looking at the peak he thought of the legend, trying to picture what had taken place here; but then he thought of the other that he had been thinking all night, and he glanced uneasily behind him.

Juan Solo watched him. "They are many hours behind," he said, "since they could not follow in the night. So, if it is not abusive to you, I say we should go quickly to the mine and leave before they arrive, continuing on in the widest circle that ends again where we started. Thus they will not know that they have been to El Sangre and left it. And later, when they see us surrounded by seven hundred bottles of mescal—" the Indian could not keep from grinning—"they will scratch their heads and turn and gaze out at the mountains that say nothing, and they will scratch their thick heads again."

Just past the canyon bend, Juan angled toward the shadowy vein of a crevice, the base overgrown with brush, which entered into a defile twisting through a squeezed-in narrowness to finally emerge in open country again at the base of the mountain.

From the ledge, Struggles' gaze lifted to the thin spire of rock, then dropped slowly, inching down with the speck that was Juan Solo descending the steep, narrow path of a rock slide that made a sweeping angle from the peak to the ledge where Struggles stood, then lost itself completely in a scatter of boulders on a bench fifty feet below. Struggles moved to the edge and glanced at the animals on the bench then on down the grade to the canyon they had left a few hours before, squinting hard, before looking back at Juan Solo.

And as the Indian reached the ledge, Struggles shook his head, then pressed his sleeve against his forehead and exhaled slowly. "I'm worn out just watching you," he said.

The Indian swung from his shoulder a blanket gathered into the shape of a sack. "Climbing for such that is up there is never wearing," he said. He untied the blanket ends and let them drop, watching Struggles, as the surgeon looked with astonishment at the dull-gleaming heap of candlesticks, chalices and crosses; all ornately tooled and some decorated with precious stones.

"These and more were placed in the sepulchre of Tomas Maria," Juan Solo said. "Along with the silver that had already been fashioned into bars when the restoration took place."

Struggles picked up a slender cruciform and ran his fingers over the baroque carvings. "It's unbelievable," he said, looking at Juan Solo. "These articles should be in a museum."

Juan Solo shook his head and there was the hint of a smile softening the straight lips of his mouth. "Then what would Tomas Maria have? These were only for if your mind doubted," he said, gathering the blanket and swinging it over his shoulder. "Now I will get your silver." And started up the slope.

Struggles felt a tingle of nervousness now; a restless urge to move about or at least face the solidness of the rock wall, as if by not seeing, the sprawling openness of the grade would not make him feel so naked. It stretched below him in a vast unmoving silence that seemed to hold time in a vacuum.

For a few minutes he watched Juan Solo almost a hundred feet above him. And when he again looked out over the slope, he saw it immediately, the thin dust thread in the distance on what only a few minutes before was a landscape as still as a painting. He watched it grow as it approached, squinting hard until he was sure, then he cupped his hands to his mouth and shouted, "Juan!" sharply. And when he saw the figure look down, he pointed out to the dust trail until he was certain Juan saw it, then went over the ledge, sliding down to the bench in a shower of loose gravel that made the animals shy at their halters and back away from the slope.

He moved them in quickly as best he could under a jutting of rock and pulled his carbine from its boot before moving back to the ledge.

* * *

THE BENCH WAS a good thousand yards up the slope from the basin floor, and from there the riders were only dots against the ragged country, indistinguishable, disappearing behind brush now and again; but finally Struggles could make out six of them following the switchbacks single-file up the grade. He pushed his carbine out over the rocks watching the front door close as they approached. There was no back door. He had no doubt as to who they were, and still they kept coming, making no attempt to stay behind cover. From a hundred yards they all looked Mexican. One of them started to wave his sombrero and suddenly there was a pistol shot from above.

Struggles looked up, going flat behind the rocks, and saw Juan Solo down on the ledge again swinging his pistol in an arc before firing twice more; and when Struggles lifted his head above the rocks, he saw only a lone figure running after the horses that were scattering far down the grade. Nothing moved along the slope where the riders had been. Beyond the scattered rock and brush, the solitary figure was slowly rounding up the horses one at a time and leading them behind the shelter of a rise.

Struggles swung his carbine across a straight line waiting for something to move. They couldn't stay down forever. But for the next few minutes nothing happened.

Then, he saw the sombrero lift hesitantly above a rock for a full second before disappearing. After a few moments, the crown was edging up again when the pistol shot sounded from above and echoed back from down the slope. The hat disappeared again and someone yelled, "Hold your fire!" and next a white cloth was waving back and forth over the rock.

A man stepped out from behind the covering holding the cloth and motioned to the side until another man moved out hesitantly to join him as he started up the grade waving the cloth. He carried only a holstered pistol, but the second man held a Winchester across the crook of his arm. They came on slowly until they were in short-pistol range.

Struggles put his sights square in the center of the first man's chest and thought how easy it would be, but then he called, "That's good enough!"

The one with the rifle hesitated, but the other didn't break his stride.

"I said that's far enough!"

He stopped then, less than fifty feet away. A willow-root straw was down close to his eyes shading his features, but you could see that he was an American. There was an easiness about him, standing in the open in a relaxed slouch; and Struggles thought, *He looks like a red-dirt farmer leaning against the corner on Saturday night. Only there's no match-stick in his mouth and a gun's only six inches from his hand.*

The one with the Winchester, a Mexican, moved up next to him and stood sideways so that the cradled barrel was pointing up to the ledge. The American followed the direction of the barrel, then looked where he thought Struggles to be.

"Tell that crazy Indian to do something with his nerves," he called.

Struggles lifted his head slightly from the rear sight. "You're the one making him nervous, not me."

"There doesn't have to be trouble—that's what I mean." He pushed the straw up from his eyes. "Why don't you come out in the open?"

Struggles' cheek pressed against the stock again. "You better get to the point pretty soon." And with the words saw the American's face break into a smile.

"Well, the point is, you're sitting on a pile of silver and I want it." His smile broadened and he added, "And the edge of the point is that we're six and you're two."

"Only when you come to get us, it's going to cost you something," Struggles said.

"Not if we sit back in the shade and wait for your tongues to swell up."

"You look a little too skinny to be good at waiting."

The American nodded to the ledge. "Ask Juan how good I am at waiting. I used up a lot of my patience while my vaqueros scratched for your sign, but I still got some left."

Struggles admitted, "It didn't take you too long at that."

"Your boy isn't the only one who knows the country." He was waving the white cloth idly. "Look," he said. "Here's how it is. You either sit and die of thirst, or else get on your mounts and ride the hell out. Of course, for my own protection I'd have to ask both of you to leave your guns behind."

Struggles said, "You don't have a high regard for our reasoning, do you?"

The man shrugged. "I'm not talking you into anything." He waited a few moments, then turned and walked down the slope. The Mexican backed down, keeping the Winchester high.

Struggles fingered the trigger lightly and wondered what that principle was based on—about not shooting a man in the back. And when the straw hat was out of range he still had not thought of it.

Through the heat of the afternoon Struggles' mind talked to him, making conversation; but always an argument resulted, and his mind was poor company because it kept telling him that he was afraid. When the heat began to lift, a breeze stirred lazily over the bench and made a faint whispering sound as it played through the crevices above. And finally, the bench lost its shape in darkness.

It was cool relief after the glaring white light of the afternoon; but with the darkness, the slope that was still a painting now came alive and was something menacing.

Struggles crawled back to the slope and stood up, cupping his hands to his mouth, and whispered, "Juan," then gritted his teeth as the word cut the silence.

He waited, but nothing happened. He brought up his hands again, but jumped back quickly as a stream of loose shale clattered down from above. And as if on signal, two rifles opened up from below. Struggles went flat and inched back to the rim as the firing kept up, spattering against the flinty slope.

* * *

WHEN IT STOPPED, he raised his head above the rocks, but there was only the darkness. *They're not a hundred feet away,* he thought. *Waiting for us to move.* He settled down again, pressing close to the rock barrier. Well, they were going to have a long wait. But now he wondered if he was alone. Since the firing there had been no sound from above. Had something happened to Juan?

Time lost its meaning after a while and became only something that dragged hope with it as it went nowhere.

Sometime after midnight, Struggles started to doze off. His head nodded and his chin was almost on his chest, but even then a consciousness warned him and he jerked his head up abruptly. He moved it from side to side now, shaking himself awake; and as his face swung to the left he saw the pinpoint of a gleam up on the mountainside.

He came to his feet, fully awake now, but blinked his eyes to make sure. The light was moving down with crawling slowness from the peak, flickering dully, but growing in intensity as it inched down the rock slide path that Juan Solo had climbed earlier.

After a few minutes Struggles saw a torch, with the flame dancing against the blackness of the slope, and as it descended to the ledge the shape of a man was illuminated weirdly in the flickering orange light it cast.

The figure moved to the edge, holding up a baroque cross whose end was the burning torch—the figure of a man wearing the coarse brown robes of a Franciscan friar.

He held the cross high overhead and spoke one sentence of Castilian, the words cold and shrill in the darkness.

"Leave this Blood of the Saint or thus your souls shall plunge to the hell of the damned!"

His arm swung back and the torch soared out into the night and down until it hit far below on the slope in a shower of bursting sparks. The figure was gone in the darkness.

Quiet settled again, but a few minutes later gunfire came from down the slope. And shortly after that, the sound of horses running hard, and dying away in the distance.

The rest of the night Struggles asked himself questions. He sat unmoving with the dead cigar stub still in his mouth and tried to think it out, applying logic. Finally he came to a conclusion. There was only one way to find out the answers to last night's mystery.

At the first sign of morning light he rose and started to climb up the slope toward the ledge.

This would answer both questions—it was the only way.

He was almost past caring whether or not the American and his men were still below. Almost. He climbed slowly, feeling the tenseness between his shoulder blades because he wasn't sure of anything. When he was nearing the rim, a hand reached down to his arm and pulled him up the rest of the way.

"Juan."

The Indian steadied him as he got to his feet. "You came with such labor, I thought you sick."

And at that moment Struggles did feel sick. Weak with relief, he was, suddenly, for only then did he realize that somehow it was all over.

He exhaled slowly and his grizzled face relaxed into a smile. He looked past Juan Solo and the smile broadened as his eyes fell on the torn blanket with the pieces of rope coiled on top of it.

"Padre, you ought to take better care of your cassock," Struggles said, nodding toward the blanket.

Juan Solo frowned. "Your words pass me," he said, looking out over the slope; and added quickly, "Let us find what occurred with the American."

Struggles was dead certain that Juan knew without even having to go down from the ledge.

Not far down the grade they found him, lying on his face with stiffened fingers clawed into the loose sand. Near his body were the ashes of the cruciform, still vaguely resembling—even as the wind began to blow it into nothingness—the shape of a cross.

Struggles said, "I take it he didn't believe in the friar, and wouldn't listen to his men who did."

Juan Solo nodded as if to say, *So you see what naturally happened,* then said, "Now there is plenty of time for your silver, Señor Doctor," and started back up the grade.

Struggles followed after him, trying to picture Tomas Maria, and thinking what a good friend the friar had in Juan Solo.

3

Three-Ten to Yuma

HE HAD PICKED up his prisoner at Fort Huachuca shortly after midnight and now, in a silent early morning mist, they approached Contention. The two riders moved slowly, one behind the other.

Entering Stockman Street, Paul Scallen glanced back at the open country with the wet haze blanketing its flatness, thinking of the long night ride from Huachuca, relieved that this much was over. When his body turned again, his hand moved over the sawed-off shotgun that was across his lap and he kept his eyes on the man ahead of him until they were near the end of the second block, opposite the side entrance of the Republic Hotel.

He said just above a whisper, though it was clear in the silence, "End of the line."

The man turned in his saddle, looking at Scallen curiously. "The jail's around on Commercial."

"I want you to be comfortable."

Scallen stepped out of the saddle, lifting a Winchester from the boot, and walked toward the hotel's side door. A figure stood in the gloom of the doorway, behind the screen, and as Scallen reached the steps the screen door opened.

"Are you the marshal?"

"Yes, sir." Scallen's voice was soft and without emotion. "Deputy, from Bisbee."

"We're ready for you. Two-oh-seven. A corner . . . fronts on Commercial." He sounded proud of the accommodation.

"You're Mr. Timpey?"

The man in the doorway looked surprised. "Yeah, Wells Fargo. Who'd you expect?"

"You might have got a back room, Mr. Timpey. One with no windows." He swung the shotgun on the man still mounted. "Step down easy, Jim."

The man, who was in his early twenties, a few years younger than Scallen, sat with one hand over the other on the saddle horn. Now he gripped the horn and swung down. When he was on the ground his hands were still close together, iron manacles holding them three chain lengths apart. Scallen motioned him toward the door with the stubby barrel of the shotgun.

"Anyone in the lobby?"

"The desk clerk," Timpey answered him, "and a man in a chair by the front door."

"Who is he?"

"I don't know. He's asleep . . . got his brim down over his eyes."

"Did you see anyone out on Commercial?"

"No . . . I haven't been out there." At first he had seemed nervous, but now he was irritated, and a frown made his face pout childishly.

Scallen said calmly, "Mr. Timpey, it was your line this man robbed. You want to see him go all the way to Yuma, don't you?"

"Certainly I do." His eyes went to the outlaw, Jim Kidd, then back to Scallen hurriedly. "But why all the melodrama? The man's under arrest—already been sentenced."

"But he's not in jail till he walks through the gates at Yuma," Scallen said. "I'm only one man, Mr. Timpey, and I've got to get him there."

"Well, dammit . . . I'm not the law! Why didn't you bring men with you? All I know is I got a wire from our Bisbee office to get a hotel room and meet you here the morning of November third. There weren't any instructions that I had to get myself deputized a marshal. That's your job."

"I know it is, Mr. Timpey," Scallen said, and smiled, though it was an effort. "But I want to make sure no one knows Jim Kidd's in Contention until after train time this afternoon."

Jim Kidd had been looking from one to the other with a faintly amused grin. Now he said to Timpey, "He means he's afraid somebody's going to jump him." He smiled at Scallen. "That marshal must've really sold you a bill of goods."

"What's he talking about?" Timpey said.

Kidd went on before Scallen could answer. "They hid me in the Huachuca lockup 'cause they knew nobody could get at me there . . . and finally the Bisbee marshal gets a plan. He and some others hopped the train in Benson last night, heading for Yuma with an army prisoner passed off as me." Kidd laughed, as if the idea were ridiculous.

"Is that right?" Timpey said.

Scallen nodded. "Pretty much right."

"How does he know all about it?"

"He's got ears and ten fingers to add with."

"I don't like it. Why just one man?"

"Every deputy from here down to Bisbee is out trying to scare up the rest of them. Jim here's the only one we caught," Scallen explained—then added, "alive."

Timpey shot a glance at the outlaw. "Is he the one who killed Dick Moons?"

"One of the passengers swears he saw who did it . . . and he didn't identify Kidd at the trial."

Timpey shook his head. "Dick drove for us a long time. You know his brother lives here in Contention. When he heard about it he almost went crazy." He hesitated, and then said again, "I don't like it."

Scallen felt his patience wearing away, but he kept his voice even when he said, "Maybe I don't either . . . but what you like and what I like aren't going to matter a whole lot, with the marshal past Tucson by now. You can grumble about it all you want, Mr. Timpey, as long as you keep it under your breath. Jim's got friends . . . and since I have to haul him clear across the territory, I'd just as soon they didn't know about it."

Timpey fidgeted nervously. "I don't see why I have to get dragged into this. My job's got nothing to do with law enforcement. . . ."

"You have the room key?"

"In the door. All I'm responsible for is the stage run between here and Tucson—"

Scallen shoved the Winchester at him. "If you'll take care of this and the horses till I get back, I'll be obliged to you . . . and I know I don't have to ask you not to mention we're at the hotel."

He waved the shotgun and nodded and Jim Kidd went ahead of him through the side door into the hotel lobby. Scallen was a stride behind him, holding the stubby shotgun close to his leg. "Up the stairs on the right, Jim."

Kidd started up, but Scallen paused to glance at the figure in the armchair near the front. He was sitting on his spine with limp hands folded on his stomach and, as Timpey had described, his hat low over the upper part of his face. You've seen people sleeping in hotel lobbies before, Scallen told himself, and followed Kidd up the stairs. He couldn't stand and wonder about it.

Room 207 was narrow and high-ceilinged, with a single window looking down on Commercial Street. An iron bed was placed the long way against one wall and extended to the right side of the window, and along the opposite wall was a dresser with washbasin and pitcher and next to it a rough-board wardrobe. An unpainted table and two straight chairs took up most of the remaining space.

"Lay down on the bed if you want to," Scallen said.

"Why don't you sleep?" Kidd asked. "I'll hold the shotgun."

The deputy moved one of the straight chairs near to the door and the other to the side of the table opposite the bed. Then he sat down, resting the shotgun on the table so that it pointed directly at Jim Kidd sitting on the edge of the bed near the window.

He gazed vacantly outside. A patch of dismal sky showed above the frame buildings across the way, but he was not sitting close enough to look directly down onto the street. He said, indifferently, "I think it's going to rain."

There was a silence, and then Scallen said, "Jim, I don't have anything against you personally . . . this is what I get paid for, but I just want it understood that if you start across the seven feet between us, I'm going to pull both triggers at once—without first asking you to stop. That clear?"

Kidd looked at the deputy marshal, then his eyes drifted out the window again. "It's kinda cold too." He rubbed his hands together and the three chain links rattled against each other. "The window's open a crack. Can I close it?"

Scallen's grip tightened on the shotgun and he brought the barrel up, though he wasn't aware of it. "If you can reach it from where you're sitting."

Kidd looked at the windowsill and said without reaching toward it, "Too far."

"All right," Scallen said, rising. "Lay back on the bed." He worked his gun belt around so that now the Colt was on his left hip.

Kidd went back slowly, smiling. "You don't take any chances, do you? Where's your sporting blood?"

"Down in Bisbee with my wife and three young-sters," Scallen told him without smiling, and moved around the table.

There were no grips on the window frame. Standing with his side to the window, facing the man on the bed, he put the heel of his hand on the bottom ledge of the frame and shoved down hard. The window banged shut and with the slam he saw Jim Kidd kicking up off of his back, his body straining to rise without his hands to help. Momentarily, Scallen hesitated and his finger tensed on the trigger. Kidd's feet were on the floor, his body swinging up and his head down to lunge from the bed. Scallen took one step and brought his knee up hard against Kidd's face.

The outlaw went back across the bed, his head striking the wall. He lay there with his eyes open looking at Scallen.

"Feel better now, Jim?"

Kidd brought his hands up to his mouth, work-ing the jaw around. "Well, I had to try you out," he said. "I didn't think you'd shoot."

"But you know I will the next time."

For a few minutes Kidd remained motionless. Then he began to pull himself straight. "I just want to sit up."

Behind the table Scallen said, "Help yourself." He watched Kidd stare out the window.

Then, "How much do you make, Marshal?"
Kidd asked the question abruptly.

"I don't think it's any of your business."

"What difference does it make?"

Scallen hesitated. "A hundred and fifty a
month," he said, finally, "some expenses, and a
dollar bounty for every arrest against a Bisbee ordi-
nance in the town limits."

Kidd shook his head sympathetically. "And you
got a wife and three kids."

"Well, it's more than a cowhand makes."

"But you're not a cowhand."

"I've worked my share of beef."

"Forty a month and keep, huh?" Kidd laughed.

"That's right, forty a month," Scallen said. He
felt awkward. "How much do you make?"

Kidd grinned. When he smiled he looked very
young, hardly out of his teens. "Name a month,"
he said. "It varies."

"But you've made a lot of money."

"Enough. I can buy what I want."

"What are you going to be wanting the next five
years?"

"You're pretty sure we're going to Yuma."

"And you're pretty sure we're not," Scallen said.
"Well, I've got two train passes and a shotgun that
says we are. What've you got?"

Kidd smiled. "You'll see." Then he said right after it, his tone changing, "What made you join the law?"

"The money," Scallen answered, and felt foolish as he said it. But he went on, "I was working for a spread over by the Pantano Wash when Old Nana broke loose and raised hell up the Santa Rosa Valley. The army was going around in circles, so the Pima County marshal got up a bunch to help out and we tracked Apaches almost all spring. The marshal and I got along fine, so he offered me a deputy job if I wanted it." He wanted to say that he started for seventy-five and worked up to the one hundred and fifty, but he didn't.

"And then someday you'll get to be marshal and make two hundred."

"Maybe."

"And then one night a drunk cowhand you've never seen will be tearing up somebody's saloon and you'll go in to arrest him and he'll drill you with a lucky shot before you get your gun out."

"So you're telling me I'm crazy."

"If you don't already know it."

Scallen took his hand off the shotgun and pulled tobacco and paper from his shirt pocket and began rolling a cigarette. "Have you figured out yet what my price is?"

Kidd looked startled, momentarily, but the grin returned. "No, I haven't. Maybe you come higher than I thought."

Scallen scratched a match across the table, lighted the cigarette, then threw it to the floor, between Kidd's boots. "You don't have enough money, Jim."

Kidd shrugged, then reached down for the cigarette. "You've treated me pretty good. I just wanted to make it easy on you."

The sun came into the room after a while. Weakly at first, cold and hazy. Then it warmed and brightened and cast an oblong patch of light between the bed and the table. The morning wore on slowly because there was nothing to do and each man sat restlessly thinking about somewhere else, though it was a restlessness within and it showed on neither of them.

The deputy rolled cigarettes for the outlaw and himself and most of the time they smoked in silence. Once Kidd asked him what time the train left. He told him shortly after three, but Kidd made no comment.

Scallen went to the window and looked out at the narrow rutted road that was Commercial Street. He pulled a watch from his vest pocket and looked at it. It was almost noon, yet there were few people about. He wondered about this and asked himself if it was unnaturally quiet for a Saturday noon in Contention . . . or if it were just his nerves. . . .

He studied the man standing under the wooden awning across the street, leaning idly against a support post with his thumbs hooked in his belt and his flat-crowned hat on the back of his head. There was something familiar about him. And each time Scallen had gone to the window—a few times during the past hour—the man had been there.

He glanced at Jim Kidd lying across the bed, then looked out the window in time to see another man moving up next to the one at the post. They stood together for the space of a minute before the second man turned a horse from the tie rail, swung up, and rode off down the street.

The man at the post watched him go and tilted his hat against the sun glare. And then it registered. With the hat low on his forehead Scallen saw him again as he had that morning. The man lying in the armchair . . . as if asleep.

He saw his wife, then, and the three youngsters and he could almost feel the little girl sitting on his lap where she had climbed up to kiss him good-bye, and he had promised to bring her something from Tucson. He didn't know why they had come to him all of a sudden. And after he had put them out of his mind, since there was no room now, there was an upset feeling inside as if he had swallowed something that would not go down all the way. It made his heart beat a little faster.

Jim Kidd was smiling up at him. "Anybody I know?"

"I didn't think it showed."

"Like the sun going down."

Scallen glanced at the man across the street and then to Jim Kidd. "Come here." He nodded to the window. "Tell me who your friend is over there."

Kidd half rose and leaned over looking out the window, then sat down again. "Charlie Prince."

"Somebody else just went for help."

"Charlie doesn't need help."

"How did you know you were going to be in Contention?"

"You told that Wells Fargo man I had friends . . . and about the posses chasing around in the hills. Figure it out for yourself. You could be looking out a window in Benson and seeing the same thing."

"They're not going to do you any good."

"I don't know any man who'd get himself killed for a hundred and fifty dollars." Kidd paused. "Especially a man with a wife and young ones. . . ."

Men rode into town in something less than an hour later. Scallen heard the horses coming up Commercial, and went to the window to see the six riders pull to a stop and range themselves in a line in the middle of the street facing the hotel.

Charlie Prince stood behind them, leaning against the post.

Then he moved away from it, leisurely, and stepped down into the street. He walked between the horses and stopped in front of them just below the window. He cupped his hands to his mouth and shouted, *"Jim!"*

In the quiet street it was like a pistol shot.

Scallen looked at Kidd, seeing the smile that softened his face and was even in his eyes. Confidence. It was all over him. And even with the manacles on, you would believe that it was Jim Kidd who was holding the shotgun.

"What do you want me to tell him?" Kidd said.

"Tell him you'll write every day."

Kidd laughed and went to the window, pushing it up by the top of the frame. It raised a few inches. Then he moved his hands under the window and it slid up all the way.

"Charlie, you go buy the boys a drink. We'll be down shortly."

"Are you all right?"

"Sure I'm all right."

Charlie Prince hesitated. "What if you don't come down? He could kill you and say you tried to break. . . . Jim, you tell him what'll happen if we hear a gun go off."

"He knows," Kidd said, and closed the window.

He looked at Scallen standing motionless with the shotgun under his arm. "Your turn, Marshal."

"What do you expect me to say?"

"Something that makes sense. You said before I didn't mean a thing to you personally—what you're doing is just a job. Well, you figure out if it's worth getting killed for. All you have to do is throw your guns on the bed and let me walk out the door and you can go back to Bisbee and arrest all the drunks you want. Nobody's going to blame you with the odds stacked seven to one. You know your wife's not going to complain. . . ."

"You should have been a lawyer, Jim."

The smile began to fade from Kidd's face. "Come on—what's it going to be?"

The door rattled with three knocks in quick succession. Abruptly the room was silent. The two men looked at each other and now the smile disappeared from Kidd's face completely.

Scallen moved to the side of the door, tiptoeing in his high-heeled boots, then pointed his shotgun toward the bed. Kidd sat down.

"Who is it?"

For a moment there was no answer. Then he heard, "Timpey."

He glanced at Kidd, who was watching him. "What do you want?"

"I've got a pot of coffee for you."

Scallen hesitated. "You alone?"

"Of course I am. Hurry up, it's hot!"

He drew the key from his coat pocket, then held the shotgun in the crook of his arm as he inserted the key with one hand and turned the knob with the other. The door opened and slammed against him, knocking him back against the dresser. He went off balance, sliding into the wardrobe, going down on his hands and knees, and the shotgun clattered across the floor to the window. He saw Jim Kidd drop to the floor for the gun. . . .

"Hold it!"

A heavyset man stood in the doorway with a Colt pointing out past the thick bulge of his stomach. "Leave that shotgun where it is." Timpey stood next to him with the coffeepot in his hand. There was coffee down the front of his suit, on the door, and on the flooring. He brushed at the front of his coat feebly, looking from Scallen to the man with the pistol.

"I couldn't help it, Marshal—he made me do it. He threatened to do something to me if I didn't."

"Who is he?"

"Bob Moons . . . you know, Dick's brother. . . ."

The heavyset man glanced at Timpey angrily. "Shut your damn whining." His eyes went to Jim Kidd and held there. "You know who I am, don't you?"

Kidd looked uninterested. "You don't resemble anybody I know."

"You didn't have to know Dick to shoot him!"

"I didn't shoot that messenger."

Scallen got to his feet, looking at Timpey. "What the hell's wrong with you?"

"I couldn't help it. He forced me."

"How did he know we were here?"

"He came in this morning talking about Dick and I felt he needed some cheering up; so I told him Jim Kidd had been tried and was being taken to Yuma and was here in town . . . on his way. Bob didn't say anything and went out, and a little later he came back with the gun."

"You damn fool." Scallen shook his head wearily.

"Never mind all the talk." Moons kept the pistol on Kidd. "I would've found him sooner or later. This way everybody gets saved a long train ride."

"You pull that trigger," Scallen said, "and you'll hang for murder."

"Like he did for killing Dick. . . ."

"A jury said he didn't do it." Scallen took a step toward the big man. "And I'm damned if I'm going to let you pass another sentence."

"You stay put or I'll pass sentence on you!"

Scallen moved a slow step nearer. "Hand me the gun, Bob."

"I'm warning you—get the hell out of the way and let me do what I came for."

"Bob, hand me the gun or I swear I'll beat you through that wall."

Scallen tensed to take another step, another slow one. He saw Moons's eyes dart from him to Kidd and in that instant he knew it would be his only chance. He lunged, swinging his coat aside with his hand, and when the hand came up it was holding a Colt. All in one motion. The pistol went up and chopped an arc across Moons's head before the big man could bring his own gun around. His hat flew off as the barrel swiped his skull and he went back against the wall heavily, then sank to the floor.

Scallen wheeled to face the window, thumbing the hammer back. But Kidd was still sitting on the edge of the bed with the shotgun at his feet.

The deputy relaxed, letting the hammer ease down. "You might have made it, that time."

Kidd shook his head. "I wouldn't have got off the bed." There was a note of surprise in his voice. "You know, you're pretty good. . . ."

At two-fifteen Scallen looked at his watch, then stood up, pushing the chair back. The shotgun was under his arm. In less than an hour they would leave the hotel, walk over Commercial to Stockman, and then up Stockman to the station. Three blocks. He wanted to go all the way. He wanted to get Jim Kidd on that train . . . but he was afraid.

He was afraid of what he might do once they were on the street. Even now his breath was short and occasionally he would inhale and let the air out slowly to calm himself. And he kept asking himself if it was worth it.

People would be in the windows and the doors, though you wouldn't see them. They'd have their own feelings and most of their hearts would be pounding . . . and they'd edge back of the door frames a little more. The man out on the street was something without a human nature or a personality of its own. He was on a stage. The street was another world.

Timpey sat on the chair in front of the door and next to him, squatting on the floor with his back against the wall, was Moons. Scallen had unloaded Moons's pistol and placed it in the pitcher behind him. Kidd was on the bed.

Most of the time he stared at Scallen. His face bore a puzzled expression, making his eyes frown, and sometimes he would cock his head as if studying the deputy from a different angle.

Scallen stepped to the window now. Charlie Prince and another man were under the awning. The others were not in sight.

"You haven't changed your mind?" Kidd asked him seriously.

Scallen shook his head.

"I don't understand you. You risk your neck to save my life, now you'll risk it again to send me to prison."

Scallen looked at Kidd and suddenly felt closer to him than any man he knew. "Don't ask me, Jim," he said, and sat down again.

After that he looked at his watch every few minutes.

At five minutes to three he walked to the door, motioning Timpey aside, and turned the key in the lock. "Let's go, Jim." When Kidd was next to him he prodded Moons with the gun barrel. "Over on the bed. Mister, if I see or hear about you on the street before train time, you'll face an attempted murder charge." He motioned Kidd past him, then stepped into the hall and locked the door.

They went down the stairs and crossed the lobby to the front door, Scallen a stride behind with the shotgun barrel almost touching Kidd's back. Passing through the doorway he said as calmly as he could, "Turn left on Stockman and keep walking. No matter what you hear, keep walking."

As they stepped out into Commercial, Scallen glanced at the ramada where Charlie Prince had been standing, but now the saloon porch was an empty shadow. Near the corner two horses stood under a sign that said EAT, in red letters; and on the other side of Stockman the signs continued, lining the rutted main street to make it seem narrower. And beneath the signs, in the shadows, nothing moved. There was a whisper of wind along the ramadas. It whipped sand specks from the street and rattled them against clapboard, and the sound was hollow and lifeless. Somewhere a screen door banged, far away.

They passed the café, turning onto Stockman. Ahead, the deserted street narrowed with distance to a dead end at the rail station—a single-story building standing by itself, low and sprawling, with most of the platform in shadow. The westbound was there, along the platform, but the engine and most of the cars were hidden by the station house. White steam lifted above the roof, to be lost in the sun's glare.

They were almost to the platform when Kidd said over his shoulder, "Run like hell while you're still able."

"Where are they?"

Kidd grinned, because he knew Scallen was afraid. "How should I know?"

"Tell them to come out in the open!"

"Tell them yourself."

"Dammit, *tell* them!" Scallen clenched his jaw and jabbed the short barrel into Kidd's back. "I'm not fooling. If they don't come out, I'll kill you!"

Kidd felt the gun barrel hard against his spine and suddenly he shouted, "Charlie!"

It echoed in the street, but after there was only the silence. Kidd's eyes darted over the shadowed porches. "Dammit, Charlie—hold on!"

Scallen prodded him up the warped plank steps to the shade of the platform and suddenly he could feel them near. "Tell him again!"

"Don't shoot, Charlie!" Kidd screamed the words.

From the other side of the station they heard the trainman's call trailing off, ". . . Gila Bend. Sentinel, Yuma!"

The whistle sounded loud, wailing, as they passed into the shade of the platform, then out again to the naked glare of the open side. Scallen squinted, glancing toward the station office, but the train dispatcher was not in sight. Nor was anyone. "It's the mail car," he said to Kidd. "The second to last one." Steam hissed from the iron cylinder of the engine, clouding that end of the platform. "Hurry it up!" he snapped, pushing Kidd along.

Then, from behind, hurried footsteps sounded on the planking, and, as the hiss of steam died away— "Stand where you are!"

The locomotive's main rods strained back, rising like the legs of a grotesque grasshopper, and the wheels moved. The connecting rods stopped on an upward swing and couplings clanged down the line of cars.

"Throw the gun away, brother!"

Charlie Prince stood at the corner of the station house with a pistol in each hand. Then he moved around carefully between the two men and the train. "Throw it far away, and unhitch your belt," he said.

"Do what he says," Kidd said. "They've got you."

The others, six of them, were strung out in the dimness of the platform shed. Grim faced, stubbles of beard, hat brims low. The man nearest Prince spat tobacco lazily.

Scallen knew fear at that moment as fear had never gripped him before; but he kept the shotgun hard against Kidd's spine. He said, just above a whisper, "Jim—I'll cut you in half!"

Kidd's body was stiff, his shoulders drawn up tightly. "Wait a minute . . ." he said. He held his palms out to Charlie Prince, though he could have been speaking to Scallen.

Suddenly Prince shouted, "Go down!"

There was a fraction of a moment of dead silence that seemed longer. Kidd hesitated. Scallen was looking at the gunman over Kidd's shoulder, seeing the two pistols. Then Kidd was gone, rolling on the planking, and the pistols were coming up, one ahead of the other. Without moving Scallen squeezed both triggers of the scattergun.

Charlie Prince was going down, holding his hands tight to his chest, as Scallen dropped the shotgun and swung around drawing his Colt. He fired hurriedly. *Wait for a target!* Words in his mind. He saw the men under the platform shed, three of them breaking for the station office, two going full length to the planks . . . one crouched, his pistol up. *That one! Get him quick!* Scallen aimed and squeezed the heavy revolver and the man went down. *Now get the hell out!*

Charlie Prince was facedown. Kidd was crawling, crawling frantically and coming to his feet when Scallen reached him. He grabbed Kidd by the collar savagely, pushing him on, and dug the pistol into his back. "Run, damn you!"

Gunfire erupted from the shed and thudded into the wooden caboose as they ran past it. The train was moving slowly. Just in front of them a bullet smashed a window of the mail car. Someone screamed, "You'll hit Jim!" There was another shot, then it was too late. Scallen and Kidd leapt up on the car platform and were in the mail car as it rumbled past the end of the station platform.

Kidd was on the floor, stretched out along a row of mail sacks. He rubbed his shoulder awkwardly with his manacled hands and watched Scallen, who stood against the wall next to the open door.

Kidd studied the deputy for some minutes. Finally he said, "You know, you really earn your hundred and a half."

Scallen heard him, though the iron rhythm of the train wheels and his breathing were loud in his temples. He felt as if all his strength had been sapped, but he couldn't help smiling at Jim Kidd. He was thinking pretty much the same thing.

4
Long Night

NEAR THE CREST of the hill, where the road climbed into the timber, he raised from the saddle wearily and turned to look back toward the small, flickering pinpoints of light.

The lights were people, and his mind gathered faces. A few he had seen less than a half hour before; but now, to Dave Boland, all of the faces were expressionless and as cold as the lights. They seemed wide-eyed and innocently, stupidly vacant.

He rode on through the timber with what was left of a hot anger, and now it was just a weariness.

He had argued all afternoon and into the evening.
Argued, reasoned, threatened and finally, pleaded.
But it had ended with "I'm sorry, I've got my supper waiting for me," and a door slammed as soon
as his back was turned.

He felt alone and inadequate, and for a moment a
panic swept him, leaving his forehead cold with per-
spiration. The worst was still ahead, telling Virginia.

Wheelock had been in the hotel dining room and
he had approached the big rancher hesitantly and
told him he was sorry to bother him. . . .

"Mr. Wheelock, I paid you prompt for that
breeding. The calf was too big, that's why it died. I
did everything I could. If you'll breed her again—"

"I heard the calf strangled. Son, when you help a
delivery, loop your rope around the head then bring
it good and tight along the jaws, and a few turns on
the forelegs if they're out." He drew circles in the
air with his fork. "Then you don't strangle them to
death." And he laughed with a mouthful of food
when he said, finally, "The breeding fee generally
doesn't include advice on how to deliver."

E. V. Timmons leaned back from the rolltop and
palmed his hands thoughtfully as if he were offering
a prayer. He looked at the ceiling for a long time with
a tragic cast to his eyes. When he spoke it was hesitantly, as if it pained him, but with conviction. . . .

"Buying trends are erratic these days, Dave. Tomorrow, demand might drop on a big item and I'd have a heavy inventory on my hands and no place to unload. It means you have to maintain a working capital."

Tom Wylie was sympathetic when he told him about most of his stock dying from rattleweed poisoning.

"That's mean stuff in March, Dave. Got to keep your stock out of it. You know, the best way to get rid of it is to cut the crowns a few inches below the soil surface. It generally won't send up new tops." He asked Boland if he had seen Timmons. And after that he kept his sympathy.

John Avery was in the hotel business. He was used to walls and space limitations. "If my cows got into rattleweed I'd put fences up to keep them the hell out. You got to organize, boy!" Avery's supper was waiting for him. . . .

Virginia would understand.

Hell, what else could she do? He saw her pale, small-boned face that now, somehow, seemed sharper and more drawn with their child only a few days or a week away. She would smile a weak smile, twisting the hem of her apron—and it would mean nothing. Virginia smiled from habit. She smiled every time he brought her bad news. But always with the same sad expression in the eyes. Sometime, in the future, perhaps there would be a real reason to smile. He wondered if she would be able to. Now, with the baby coming . . .

Virginia had waited tables in a restaurant in Sudan because she had to support herself after her folks died suddenly. She was a great kidder and all the riders liked her. Broadminded, they said. He used to pass through Sudan a few times a year when most of the Company herds were grazed near the Canadian. After a while, he went out of his way and even made excuses to go there. She never kidded with him . . .

When he told the others about it, they said, "She's a nice girl—but who wants a nice girl? You get bone-tired pushing steers from the Nueces to Dodge; but, son, you can throw off along the way anytime you want—"

It had been raining hard for the past few minutes when finally he led his mare into the long, rickety shed, unsaddled and pitch-forked some hay.

The rain, he thought, shaking his head. The one thing I don't need is rain. He tried to see humor in it, though it was an irritation. Like an annoying, tickling fly lighting on a broken leg.

He walked up the slight grade toward the dim shape of the adobe house, passing the empty chicken coops, then skirted Virginia's vegetable garden, moving around toward the front of the house. He saw a light through a curtained side window. At the front of the house he called, "It's me," so as not to startle her, then lifted the latch on the door and pushed in.

Virginia Boland stood next to the oilcloth-covered table. She twisted the hem of her apron—she did it deliberately, her fingers tensed white straining at the material—and her eyes were wide. No smile softened the pale, oval face. Her dark dress was ill-fitting about her narrow shoulders and bosom as if it were sizes too large, then rounded, bulging with her pregnancy to lose any shape it might have had before.

Boland said, taking his hat off, "I guess I don't have to tell you what happened."

"Dave—" Her voice was small, and now almost a whisper. Her eyes still wide.

He came out of his coat and brushed it half-heartedly before throwing it to a chair.

"I saw all of them, Ginny."

"Dave— "

He looked at her curiously now across the few feet that separated them. . . . There was something in her voice. And suddenly he knew she wasn't saying his name in answer to his words. He moved to her quickly and held her by the shoulders.

"Is it time? Are you ready now?"

She shook her head, looking at him imploringly as if she were saying something with her eyes, but she didn't speak.

She didn't have to.

"Hello, Davie boy." The voice came from behind Virginia.

He stood in the doorway of the partitioned bedroom with the curtain draped over his shoulder. The white cloth dropped to the floor showing only part of him; damp and grimy, trail dust streaked and smeared over clothes that had not been changed for days. A yellow slicker was draped over his lower arm and his hand would have gone unnoticed if the long pistol barrel were not sticking out from the raincoat.

"Been a long time, hasn't it!" he said, and came into the room carefully, lifting the slicker from his arm to drape it over a straight chair. "I almost didn't recognize little Ginny with her new shape." He grinned, winking at Boland. "You didn't waste any time, did you?"

Boland stared at the man self-consciously, feeling a nervousness that was edged with fear, but he made himself smile.

"Jeffy, I almost didn't recognize you," he said.

"Wait'll you see Red." His head turned to the side and he called to the bedroom, "Red, come on out!"

Boland looked toward the curtained doorway and then to the dirt-caked figure next to him. "I wouldn't have known you by sight, but your voice—"

"You didn't forget that Cimarron crossing two years ago, did you?"

"Of course I remember," Boland said. "You saved my life." He tried to show friendship and appreciation at the same time and smiled when he said, "What are you doing here, Jeffy?"

"You're a regular babe in the woods, aren't you?" His head turned again. "Red! Dammit!"

He hesitated in the doorway, leaning against the partition, and then came into the room, straining to move his legs and holding his arms tight to his stomach as if his insides would fall out with a heavy step. He was as filthy as the other man, but his grime-streaked, bearded face was sickly white and his jaw muscles clenched as he eased himself down onto the cot which stood against the side wall nearer the two men.

He leaned back until his head and shoulders were against the adobe, then blew his breath out in a low groan. He held his right elbow to his side protectingly, and from under his arm a dark, wet stain reached in a smear almost to the buttons on his shirt.

Boland looked at Jeffy who was leaning against their small table with his arms folded and the pistol pointing up past his shoulder and heard him say, "Red's sick."

He glanced at his wife who was holding her hands close to her waist and then he moved closer to the cot. "How are you, Red?"

The man shook his head wearily, but didn't speak.

Leaning over him, Boland said in subdued surprise, "That's a gunshot wound!"

Jeffy came off the table now and pushed Boland away from the cot. "You want to know every thing," he said, and glanced down at Red. "Keep your eyes open. You're not that bad hurt."

"What's the matter with you!" Boland flared. "He's been shot clean through."

Jeffy shrugged. "Tell him something he doesn't know."

Boland turned on him angrily. "What happened! If you're going to dirty up my house, you're going to tell me what happened!"

"You're forgetting about that Cimarron crossing." Jeffy smiled. He was near forty with a thin, wizened face made lopsided by a tobacco wad; and now he took off his shapeless hat to show a receding hairline and a high, white forehead that looked obscenely naked because of its whiteness. He looked at Boland's wife, wiping his mouth with the back of his hand.

"Honey, he ever tell you how I pulled him out from under the cows? Deep water after a flash flood and they was millin' in the stream—" He grinned at her as if there was a secret between them. "You'd still be shaking your tail in that Sudan hash-house if it wasn't for me."

"Saving my life doesn't bless anything you've got

to say to my wife." Boland had felt the temper hot in his face, but he calmed himself. Now his voice was lower, but there was an edge to it still.

"And it doesn't give you leave to walk in my house with your gun out and start pushing everybody around. I know you're in some trouble. With your dirty mind and Red's drinking it could be almost anything. Now I'm telling you, Jeffy, start acting right or move on."

Jeffy shook his head sadly. "That's some way to talk after all the time Red and me and you bunked together."

"What did you do, Jeffy?"

There was a pause and his face became serious. "Held up a man and Red shot him when he went for his gun."

"Where'd it happen?"

As suddenly as he had become serious, his face grinned again and he said, "You always did have a long nose." He looked over to the cot and said, "Red!" surprising the man's eyes open.

"I'm not going to tell you again. Keep your eyes open." He lifted his slicker from the chair and shrugged an arm into it. "Pull your gun and hold it on them, while I take a look around. I might even go all the way toward town, so don't get jumpy if I'm gone a couple hours."

He started for the door, buttoning the slicker

with one hand, then looked at Virginia. "Honey, you have some coffee on for when I get back. Like you used to." He grinned at her showing tobacco-yellowed teeth and shook his head reminiscently. "You sure used to throw it around in that café."

She looked away from him to her husband. Neither of them spoke.

"Your joining society's changed you, honey. There was a time when we couldn't shut you up." They heard the rain when he opened the door, then the sound was closed off again and he was gone.

In the room's abrupt silence Red drew his pistol, but his hand fell to the cot and the fingers closed on the handle loosely. He did not cock it.

Looking at him, Boland tried to picture him killing a man. Neither he nor Jeffy were ever good citizens, he thought. But they never robbed or killed before. He had worked with them for a couple of years when he first started riding for the T. & N. M. Cattle Company and he had not particularly liked them then; but his dislikes were based on small, personal things—Jeffy always making dirty remarks, and Red getting sloppy drunk any chance he had. Both had been lazy and never did any more than they had to.

And now—they had to flop themselves right on top of his other troubles.

Virginia moved over to the stove and lighted the fire under the coffeepot. She said to him, "Are you hungry, Dave?"

He shook his head. "Not very." *And I've got to worry about Ginny on top of all of it.* And then he thought: *or, are you feeling sorry for yourself?*

"Are you?" Her head nodded to the man on the cot.

"I don't think I'd hold it."

Boland asked him now, "When were you shot, Red?"

"Yesterday, in Clovis. Somebody musta recognized me and told the marshal. He hit me by surprise."

"Right after you killed this man?"

"Hell, that was months ago in Dodge. We been hiding since. Went into Clovis yesterday for grub and somebody seen us." He was breathing easier and went on, "We lost them last night. Damn marshal hit me by surprise—"

Boland said, "I suppose you were drunk in Dodge."

Red grinned sheepishly. "Fact is, I don't even remember shootin' the man."

"But Jeffy told you you did."

"Yeah, Jeffy said I was actin' mean and—"

"And lost your nerve and shot him when you didn't have to."

Red looked surprised. "Yeah. That's just what he said."

Boland waited, watching the man think it over. Then, "You starting to get any notions in your head?" It occurred to him then for the first time. He had been thinking Red was a damn fool hiding all that time because of Jeffy—unless his face was plastered all over the country. Otherwise, how would anyone in Clovis have known him? Then it hit him: a reward!

Virginia moved past him holding the coffeepot and a porcelain cup. She handed the cup to Red. "Try some coffee. Maybe you'll feel better."

"I don't think I'd hold it."

"Well, try, anyway."

He held the cup over his lap in his left hand and she leaned closer to pour the coffee. Suddenly she moved the pot to the side and emptied the scalding coffee on Red's gun hand.

His hand went up as he screamed and the gun flew over the foot of the cot, and in the instant she pushed the palm of her hand over his mouth forcing his head against the wall and muffling his scream.

Boland came up with the gun. He did it without thinking; and now, as he leveled it in Red's face he looked at Virginia with disbelief in his wide-open eyes. They followed her as she moved across the room, replaced the coffeepot on the stove and returned to stand awkwardly near the cot. She bit her lower lip nervously, watching the man.

The violent motion had ripped open his wound and now it was bleeding again. He hugged his arm to his side, groaning, with his scalded hand held limply in front of him.

Virginia's head lowered closer to his and she said, "I'm sorry," embarrassedly.

For another moment Boland continued to stare at her, but now with curiosity in place of surprise, as if he wasn't quite sure he knew this woman he had married.

He handed her the pistol. "Want me to cock it?"

"I can do that."

"If he budges, shoot him quick."

He moved toward the door and hesitated momentarily before turning back to Virginia. He kissed her mouth softly and looking into her face as he drew away, her features seemed not so sharp and pointed. And there was more color to her skin. He moved to the door anxiously, but glanced at her again before going out.

The rain had worn itself to a cold drizzle and there was no moon to make shadows in the blackness. He moved around the house slowly, cautiously, and hugged the adobe as he passed the garden. His pistol was in the saddlebag hanging in the barn-shed and now he thought: why in hell didn't I bring it in!

No, then Jeffy would have it now. But he wouldn't know it was in the saddlebag. I've to get the gun—and then Jeffy. But where is he?

He reached the back of the house and crouched down in the dead silence, looking in the direction of the barn-shed. He waited, listening for a sound, and after a few minutes he could make out an oblong, hazy outline. He thought of Virginia now and he didn't feel so alone. Even the business of the afternoon, when it crept into his mind, didn't cause a sinking feeling, and he went over everything calmly. It puzzled him, because he was used to feeling alone. He thought of the reward again. . . .

He arose abruptly and sprinted across the back section toward the barn. He ran half-crouched, even though it was dark. At the side of the doorway, he pressed his back to the wall and listened. He waited again, then slowly inched his head past the opening. It was darker within. He stepped inside quickly and as he did, felt the gun barrel jab into his spine.

"You must be dumber than I thought you were," Jeffy said.

★ ★ ★

VIRGINIA BACKED toward the table slowly, her free hand feeling for the edge, and when her fingers touched the smooth oilcloth she moved around it so that now the table was between her and the man on the cot. She did not take her eyes from the sprawled figure as she reached behind for the chair. There was a flutter of movement within her and she held the pistol with both hands, sitting down quickly. She trained the front sight on the man and saw it tremble slightly against the background of his body.

He closed his eyes suddenly, grinding his teeth together, and when he opened them they were dark hollows in his bloodless face. His mouth opened as if he would say something, but he blew his breath out wearily and moved a boot until it slid off the cot to the floor. His teeth clenched as it hit the flooring.

He brought his left hand over to the wound, his face tightening as his fingers touched the blood-smear of shirt that was stuck fast to the wound. It was still bleeding and now a dark stain was forming on the light wool blanket that covered the mattress.

She watched the stain spreading on the blanket where it touched his side and again she felt the squirm of life within her. She felt suddenly faint.

She remembered the afternoon her mother had given her the blanket and how she'd folded it into the chest with her linens and materials. She had seated herself on the chest then and clasped her hands contentedly, listing her possessions in her mind and thinking, smiling: now all I need is a husband. She had giggled then, she remembered.

For the bed, they used Dave's heavy army blankets. The cot served as a sofa and deserved something bright and dressy enough for the front room.

Red lifted his boot to the cot, and stretched it out tensely, and as the heel slid over the blanket a streak of sand-colored clay followed the heel in a thin crumbling line.

And then she no longer recognized the blanket. It became something else with this man sprawled on top of it. It became part of him with his blood staining it. And she saw the man and the blanketed cot as one. The wound was in the center. It was the focal point.

His face grimaced again with the pain and he groaned.

She said softly, "Haven't you done anything for it?"

He was breathing through his mouth as if his lungs were worn out and there was a pause before he said, "I stuffed my bandanna inside till it got soaked through, then I threw it away."

She stared at the bloodstain without speaking. Then, suddenly, she laid the pistol on the table and went over to the stove.

Red watched her pour water from a kettle into a shallow, porcelain pan before reaching for a towel that hung from a wall rack. His eyes drifted to the gun on the table and his body strained as if he would rise, but as Virginia turned and moved toward him, he relaxed.

She caught the slight movement and stopped halfway to the cot, her eyes going from the man to the table. She hesitated for a moment, then went on to the cot where she kneeled down, placing the pan on the floor.

She poured water on the wound and pulled at the shirt gently, working it loose. When it was free she tore the shirt up to the armpit, exposing the raw wound. It looked swollen and tender, fire-red around the puncture then darkening into a surrounding purplish-blue.

She looked into his face briefly. "Didn't your *friend* offer to help you?"

"He had to worry about getting us out."

"After he got you in."

Red said, irritably, "I've got a mind of my own."

She held the wet cloth to the wound then took it away, wringing the stained water from it. "Then why don't you use it?" she said calmly.

Red looked at her hard, then flared, "Maybe Jeffy was right. Maybe since you quit swingin' your tail in a hash-house, all of a sudden you're somebody else."

Virginia's head remained lowered over the pan as she rinsed out the cloth, squeezing it into the water. "You don't have any cause to talk like that."

She went to the wall rack and brought back a dry

cloth and neither of them spoke as she folded it and pressed it gently against the wound.

And as she did this, Red's eyes lowered to the streak of clay on the blanket and he brushed it off carefully. He looked at the bloodstain and said in a low voice, "I'm sorry about your cover." He was silent for a moment then said, almost dazedly, "I'm going to die—"

She made no answer and now his eyes lifted to her faded blond hair and then over her head to roam about the room. He was thinking about the soiled blanket and now he saw the raveling poplin curtains that looked flimsy and ridiculous next to the drab adobe. On the board partition there was a print of a girl in a ballet costume, soft-shadowed color against the rough boards. And over by the far wall was the grotesquely fat stove, its flue reaching up through the low ceiling.

He said, "You got it pretty hard, haven't you?"

She hesitated before saying, "We get by."

"Well," he said, glancing around again, "I wouldn't say you had the world by the tail."

Virginia looked up quickly. There was a rattling of knocks on the door and from outside she heard, "Honey, give that gun back to Red like a good girl."

* * *

JEFFY CAME THROUGH the doorway prodding Boland before him. He glared at Red who was holding his gun on his lap carelessly. "You're some watchdog."

Red said nothing, but then he gagged as if he would be sick. He breathed hard with his mouth open to catch his breath and then seemed to sag within himself. His eyes were open, but lifeless.

"It's a good thing I tested you out, Red."

Red was silent for a moment. Then he said, "Jeffy, did I shoot that man in Dodge?"

"I told you you did." He looked at Red curiously.

"But I don't remember doing it."

"How many things you ever done do you remember?"

"I thought I'd remember killing a man."

Jeffy rolled the tobacco on his tongue, looking around the room. Then he shrugged and sent a stream of it to the floor. "I'm not going to argue with you, Red. I don't have time." He glanced at Virginia. "Honey, how'd you like to go for a ride?"

There was a silence then, and Jeffy laughed to fill it. "You don't think I'm riding out of here without some protection!" He looked at Boland. "Davie, would you take a pot at me with your woman hangin' onto my cantle?"

Boland's face was white. For a moment there had been a fury inside of him, but his brain had fought it and now he felt only panic. There was a plea in his voice when he said, "My wife's going to have a baby."

Jeffy grinned at him. "All the more reason."

"Jeffy."

He glanced at Red who seemed suddenly wide awake.

"Jeffy, you're just scaring, aren't you?"

"What do you think?"

He looked at him, squinting, as if he were trying to read his mind. "You'd take that girl on horseback the way she is?"

"Red, if I had a violin I'd accompany you." He started toward Virginia.

And with his movement the gun turned in Red's lap, and the room filled with the roar as it went off. He cocked to fire again, but there was no need. He looked at Jeffy lying facedown on the floor and said incredulously, "He would have done it!"

He let the pistol fall to the floor. "There," he said to Virginia. "Keep your coffeepot away from here."

Boland looked at Jeffy and then picked up the pistol. Virginia smiled at him wearily and sat down at the table, propping her elbows on it. He said to her, "Maybe you better get some sleep."

"Dave."

He turned to Red.

"I'm going to die, Dave."

Boland remained silent.

"Do me a favor and don't holler law until the morning. Then it won't matter."

"All right, Red." Then he said, "I don't want to sound like a gravepicker, but how much have you and Jeffy got on your heads?"

Red looked at him, surprised. "Reward?"

Boland nodded.

"Why, nothin'. What made you think so?"

"You said somebody identified you in Clovis."

"Well, it was probably somebody used to know us."

Now that he had asked him, Boland was embarrassed. But, strangely, there was no disappointment and at that moment it surprised him. He grinned at Virginia. "I guess you don't get anything for nothing."

She smiled back at him and didn't look so tired. "You should know that by now."

For a few minutes there was silence. They could hear Red's breathing, but it was soft and even. Suddenly, Boland said, "Ginny, you know I haven't been home more'n an hour!"

Virginia nodded. "And it seemed like the whole, long night." Her eyes smiled at him and she said, softly, "When you're telling our grandchildren about it, maybe you can stretch it a little bit."

5

The Captives

Chapter One

HE COULD HEAR the stagecoach, the faraway creaking and the muffled rumble of it, and he was thinking: It's almost an hour early. Why should it be if it left Contention on schedule?

His name was Pat Brennan. He was lean and almost tall, with a deeply tanned, pleasant face beneath the straight hat brim low over his eyes, and he stood next to his saddle, which was on the ground, with the easy, hip-shot slouch of a rider. A Henry rifle was in his right hand and he was squinting into the sun glare, looking up the grade to the rutted road that came curving down through the spidery Joshua trees.

He lowered the Henry rifle, stock down, and let it fall across the saddle, and kept his hand away from the Colt holstered on his right leg. A man could get shot standing next to a stage road out in the middle of nowhere with a rifle in his hand.

Then, seeing the coach suddenly against the sky, billowing dust hanging over it, he felt relief and smiled to himself and raised his arm to wave as the coach passed through the Joshuas.

As the pounding wood, iron, and three-team racket of it came swaying toward him, he raised both arms and felt a sudden helplessness as he saw that the driver was making no effort to stop the teams. Brennan stepped back quickly, and the coach rushed past him, the driver, alone on the boot, bending forward and down to look at him.

Brennan cupped his hands and called, *"Rin-toooon!"*

The driver leaned back with the reins high and through his fingers, his boot pushing against the brake lever, and his body half turned to look back over the top of the Concord. Brennan swung the saddle up over his shoulder and started after the coach as it ground to a stop.

He saw the company name, HATCH & HODGES, and just below it, *Number 42* stenciled on the varnished door; then from a side window, he saw a man staring at him irritably as he approached. Behind the man he caught a glimpse of a woman with soft features and a small, plumed hat and eyes that looked away quickly as Brennan's gaze passed them going up to Ed Rintoon, the driver.

"Ed, for a minute I didn't think you were going to stop."

Rintoon, a leathery, beard-stubbled man in his mid-forties, stood with one knee on the seat and looked down at Brennan with only faint surprise.

"I took you for being up to no good, standing there waving your arms."

"I'm only looking for a lift a ways."

"What happened to you?"

Brennan grinned and his thumb pointed back vaguely over his shoulder. "I was visiting Tenvoorde to see about buying some yearling stock and I lost my horse to him on a bet."

"Driver!"

Brennan turned. The man who had been at the window was now leaning halfway out of the door and looking up at Rintoon.

"I'm not paying you to pass the time of day

with"—he glanced at Brennan—"with everybody we meet."

Rintoon leaned over to look down at him. "Willard, you ain't even part right, since you ain't the man that pays me."

"I chartered this coach, and you along with it!" He was a young man, hatless, his long hair mussed from the wind. Strands of it hung over his ears, and his face was flushed as he glared at Rintoon. "When I pay for a coach I expect the service that goes with it."

Rintoon said, "Willard, you calm down now."

"Mr. Mims!"

Rintoon smiled faintly, glancing at Brennan. "Pat, I'd like you to meet Mr. Mims." He paused, adding, "He's a bookkeeper."

Brennan touched the brim of his hat toward the coach, seeing the woman again. She looked to be in her late twenties and her eyes now were wide and frightened and not looking at him.

His glance went to Willard Mims. Mims came out of the doorway and stood pointing a finger up at Rintoon.

"Brother, you're through! I swear to God this is your last run on any line in the Territory!"

Rintoon eased himself down until he was half sitting on the seat. "You wouldn't kid me."

"You'll see if I'm kidding!"

Rintoon shook his head. "After ten years of faithful service the boss will be sorry to see me go."

Willard Mims stared at him in silence. Then he said, his voice calmer, "You won't be so sure of yourself after we get to Bisbee."

Ignoring him, Rintoon turned to Brennan. "Swing that saddle up here."

"You hear what I said?" Willard Mims flared.

Reaching down for the saddle horn as Brennan lifted it, Rintoon answered, "You said I'd be sorry when we got to Bisbee."

"You remember that!"

"I sure will. Now you get back inside, Willard." He glanced at Brennan. "You get in there, too, Pat."

Willard Mims stiffened. "I'll remind you again—this is *not* the passenger coach."

Brennan was momentarily angry, but he saw the way Rintoon was taking this and he said calmly, "You want me to walk? It's only fifteen miles to Sasabe."

"I didn't say that," Mims answered, moving to the coach door. "If you want to come, get up on the boot." He turned to look at Brennan as he pulled himself up on the foot rung. "If we'd wanted company we'd have taken the scheduled run. That clear enough for you?"

Glancing at Rintoon, Brennan swung the Henry rifle up to him and said, "Yes, sir," not looking at

Mims; and he winked at Rintoon as he climbed the wheel to the driver's seat.

A moment later they were moving, slowly at first, bumping and swaying; then the road seemed to become smoother as the teams pulled faster.

Brennan leaned toward Rintoon and said, in the noise, close to the driver's grizzled face, "I wondered why the regular stage would be almost an hour early, Ed, I'm obliged to you."

Rintoon glanced at him. "Thank Mr. Mims."

"Who is he, anyway?"

"Old man Gateway's son-in-law. Married the boss's daughter. Married into the biggest copper claim in the country."

"The girl with him his wife?"

"Doretta," Rintoon answered. "That's Gateway's daughter. She was scheduled to be an old maid till Willard come along and saved her from spinsterhood. She's plain as a 'dobe wall."

Brennan said, "But not too plain for Willard, eh?"

Rintoon gave him a side glance. "Patrick, there ain't nothing plain about old man Gateway's holdings. That's the thing. Four years ago he bought a half interest in the Montezuma Copper Mine for two hundred and fifty thousand dollars, and he's got it back triple since then. Can you imagine anyone having that much money?"

Brennan shook his head. "Where'd he get it, to start?"

"They say he come from money and made more by using the brains God gave him, investing it."

Brennan shook his head again. "That's too much money, Ed. Too much to have to worry about."

"Not for Willard, it ain't," Rintoon said. "He started out as a bookkeeper with the company. Now he's general manager—since the wedding. The old man picked Willard because he was the only one around he thought had any polish, and he knew if he waited much longer he'd have an old maid on his hands. And, Pat"—Rintoon leaned closer—"Willard don't talk to the old man like he does to other people."

"She didn't look so bad to me," Brennan said.

"You been down on Sasabe Creek too long." Rintoon glanced at him again. "What were you saying about losing your horse to Tenvoorde?"

"Oh, I went to see him about buying some year-lings—"

"On credit," Rintoon said.

Brennan nodded. "Though I was going to pay him some of it cash. I told him to name a fair interest rate and he'd have it in two years. But he said no. Cash on the line. No cash, no yearlings. I needed three hundred to make the deal, but I only had fifty. Then when I was going he said, 'Patrick'—

you know how he talks—'I'll give you a chance to get your yearlings free,' and all the time he's eyeing this claybank mare I had along. He said, 'You bet your mare and your fifty dollars cash, I'll put up what yearlings you need, and we'll race your mare against one of my string for the winner.' "

Ed Rintoon said, "And you lost."

"By a country mile."

"Pat, that don't sound like you. Why didn't you take what your fifty would buy and get on home?"

"Because I needed these yearlings plus a good seed bull. I could've bought the bull, but I wouldn't have had the yearlings to build on. That's what I told Mr. Tenvoorde. I said, 'This deal's as good as the stock you're selling me. If you're taking that kind of money for a seed bull and yearlings, then you know they can produce. You're sure of getting your money.' "

"You got stock down on your Sasabe place," Rintoon said.

"Not like you think. They wintered poorly and I got a lot of building to do."

"Who's tending your herd now?"

"I still got those two Mexican boys."

"You should've known better than to go to Tenvoorde."

"I didn't have a chance. He's the only man close enough with the stock I want."

"But a bet like that—how could you fall into it? You know he'd have a pony to outstrip yours."

"Well, that was the chance I had to take."

They rode along in silence for a few minutes before Brennan asked, "Where they coming from?"

Rintoon grinned at him. "Their honeymoon. Willard made the agent put on a special run just for the two of them. Made a big fuss while Doretta tried to hide her head."

"Then"—Brennan grinned—"I'm obliged to Mr. Mims, else I'd still be waiting back there with my saddle and my Henry."

Later on, topping a rise that was thick with jack pine, they were suddenly in view of the Sasabe station and the creek beyond it, as they came out of the trees and started down the mesquite-dotted sweep of the hillside.

Rintoon checked his timepiece. The regular run was due here at five o'clock. He was surprised to see that it was only ten minutes after four. He remembered then, his mind picturing Willard Mims as he chartered the special coach.

Brennan said, "I'm getting off here at Sasabe."

"How'll you get over to your place?"

"Hank'll lend me a horse."

As they drew nearer, Rintoon was squinting, studying the three adobe houses and the corral in back. "I don't see anybody," he said. "Hank's usually out in the yard. Him or his boy."

Brennan said, "They don't expect you for an hour. That's it."

"Man, we make enough noise for somebody to come out."

Rintoon swung the teams toward the adobes, slowing them as Brennan pushed his boot against the brake lever, and they came to a stop exactly even with the front of the main adobe.

"Hank!"

Rintoon looked from the door of the adobe out over the yard. He called the name again, but there was no answer. He frowned. "The damn place sounds deserted," he said.

Brennan saw the driver's eyes drop to the sawed-off shotgun and Brennan's Henry on the floor of the boot, and then he was looking over the yard again.

"Where in hell would Hank've gone to?"

A sound came from the adobe. A boot scraping—that or something like it—and the next moment a man was standing in the open doorway. He was bearded, a dark beard faintly streaked with gray and in need of a trim. He was watching them calmly, almost indifferently, and leveling a Colt at them at the same time.

He moved out into the yard and now another

man, armed with a shotgun, came out of the adobe. The bearded one held his gun on the door of the coach. The shotgun was leveled at Brennan and Rintoon.

"You-all drop your guns and come on down." He wore range clothes, soiled and sun bleached, and he held the shotgun calmly as if doing this was not something new. He was younger than the bearded one by at least ten years.

Brennan raised his revolver from its holster and the one with the shotgun said, "Gently, now," and grinned as Brennan dropped it over the wheel.

Rintoon, not wearing a handgun, had not moved.

"If you got something down in that boot," the one with the shotgun said to him, "haul it out."

Rintoon muttered something under his breath. He reached down and took hold of Brennan's Henry rifle lying next to the sawed-off shotgun, his finger slipping through the trigger guard. He came up with it hesitantly, and Brennan whispered, barely moving his lips, "Don't be crazy."

Standing up, turning, Rintoon hesitated again, then let the rifle fall. "That all you got?"

Rintoon nodded. "That's all."

"Then come on down."

Rintoon turned his back. He bent over to climb down, his foot reaching for the wheel below, and his hand closed on the sawed-off shotgun. Brennan whispered, "Don't do it!"

Rintoon mumbled something that came out as a growl. Brennan leaned toward him as if to give him a hand down. "You got two shots. What if there're more than two of them?"

Rintoon grunted, "Look out, Pat!" His hand gripped the shotgun firmly.

Then he was turning, jumping from the wheel, the stubby scattergun flashing head-high—and at the same moment a single revolver shot blasted the stillness. Brennan saw Rintoon crumple to the ground, the shotgun falling next to him, and he was suddenly aware of powder smoke and a man framed in the window of the adobe.

The one with the shotgun said, "Well, that just saves some time," and he glanced around as the third man came out of the adobe. "Chink, I swear you hit him in midair."

"I was waiting for that old man to pull something," said the one called Chink. He wore two low-slung, crossed cartridge belts and his second Colt was still in its holster.

Brennan jumped down and rolled Rintoon over gently, holding his head off the ground. He looked at the motionless form and then at Chink. "He's dead."

Chink stood with his legs apart and looked down at Brennan indifferently. "Sure he is."

"You didn't have to kill him."

Chink shrugged. "I would've, sooner or later."

"Why?"

"That's the way it is."

The man with the beard had not moved. He said now, quietly, "Chink, you shut your mouth." Then he glanced at the man with the shotgun and said, in the same tone, "Billy-Jack, get them out of there," and nodded toward the coach.

★

Chapter Two

Kneeling next to Rintoon, Brennan studied them. He watched Billy-Jack open the coach door, saw his mouth soften to a grin as Doretta Mims came out first. Her eyes went to Rintoon, but shifted away quickly. Willard Mims hesitated, then stepped down, stumbling in his haste as Billy-Jack pointed the shotgun at him. He stood next to his wife and stared unblinkingly at Rintoon's body.

That one, Brennan was thinking, looking at the man with the beard—that's the one to watch. He's calling it, and he doesn't look as though he gets excited. . . . And the one called Chink. . . .

Brennan's eyes went to him. He was standing hip-cocked, his hat on the back of his head and the drawstring from it pulled tight beneath his lower lip, his free hand fingering the string idly, the other hand holding the long-barreled .44 Colt, pointed down but cocked.

He wants somebody to try something, Brennan thought. He's itching for it. He wears two guns and he thinks he's good. Well, maybe he is. But he's young, the youngest of the three, and he's anxious. His gaze stayed on Chink and it went through his mind: Don't even reach for a cigarette when he's around.

The one with the beard said, "Billy-Jack, get up on top of the coach."

Brennan's eyes raised, watching the man step from the wheel hub to the boot and then kneel on the driver's seat. He's number-three man, Brennan thought. He keeps looking at the woman. But don't bet him short. He carries a big-gauge gun.

"Frank, there ain't nothing up here but an old saddle."

The one with the beard—Frank Usher—raised his eyes. "Look under it."

"Ain't nothing there either."

Usher's eyes went to Willard Mims, then swung slowly to Brennan. "Where's the mail?"

"I wouldn't know," Brennan said.

Frank Usher looked at Willard Mims again. "You tell me."

"This isn't the stage," Willard Mims said hesitantly. His face relaxed then, almost to the point of smiling. "You made a mistake. The regular stage isn't due for almost an hour." He went on, excitement rising in his voice, "That's what you want, the stage that's due here at five. This is one I chartered." He smiled now. "See, me and my wife are just coming back from a honeymoon and, you know—"

Frank Usher looked at Brennan. "Is that right?"

"Of course it is!" Mims's voice rose. "Go in and check the schedule."

"I'm asking this man."

Brennan shrugged. "I wouldn't know."

"He don't know anything," Chink said.

Billy-Jack came down off the coach and Usher said to him, "Go in and look for a schedule." He nodded toward Doretta Mims. "Take that woman with you. Have her put some coffee on, and something to eat."

Brennan said, "What did you do with Hank?"

Frank Usher's dull eyes moved to Brennan. "Who's he?"

"The station man here."

Chink grinned and waved his revolver, pointing it off beyond the main adobe. "He's over yonder in the well."

Usher said, "Does that answer it?"

"What about his boy?"

"He's with him," Usher said. "Anything else?"

Brennan shook his head slowly. "That's enough." He knew they were both dead and suddenly he was very much afraid of this dull-eyed, soft-voiced man with the beard; it took an effort to keep himself calm. He watched Billy-Jack take Doretta by the arm. She looked imploringly at her husband, holding back, but he made no move to help her. Billy-Jack jerked her arm roughly and she went with him.

Willard Mims said, "He'll find the schedule. Like I said, it's due at five o'clock. I can see how you made the mistake"—Willard was smiling—"thinking we were the regular stage. Hell, we were just going home . . . down to Bisbee. You'll see, five o'clock sharp that regular passenger-mail run'll pull in."

"He's a talker," Chink said.

Billy-Jack appeared in the doorway of the adobe. "Frank, five o'clock, sure as hell!" He waved a sheet of yellow paper.

"See!" Willard Mims was grinning excitedly. "Listen, you let us go and we'll be on our way"— his voice rose—"and I swear to God we'll never breathe we saw a thing."

Chink shook his head. "He's somethin'."

"Listen, I swear to God we won't tell *anything*!"

"I know you won't," Frank Usher said. He

looked at Brennan and nodded toward Mims. "Where'd you find him?"

"We just met."

"Do you go along with what he's saying?"

"If I said yes," Brennan answered, "you wouldn't believe me. And you'd be right."

A smile almost touched Frank Usher's mouth. "Dumb even talking about it, isn't it?"

"I guess it is," Brennan said.

"You know what's going to happen to you?" Usher asked him tonelessly.

Brennan nodded, without answering.

Frank Usher studied him in silence. Then, "Are you scared?"

Brennan nodded again. "Sure I am."

"You're honest about it. I'll say that for you."

"I don't know of a better time to be honest," Brennan said.

Chink said, "That damn well's going to be chock full."

Willard Mims had listened with disbelief, his eyes wide. Now he said hurriedly, "Wait a minute! What're you listening to him for? I told you, I swear to God I won't say one word about this. If you don't trust him, then keep him here! I don't know this man. I'm not speaking for him, anyway."

"I'd be inclined to trust him before I would you," Frank Usher said.

"He's got nothing to do with it! We picked him up out on the desert!"

Chink raised his .44 waist high, looking at Willard Mims, and said, "Start running for that well and see if you can make it."

"Man, be reasonable!"

Frank Usher shook his head. "You aren't leaving, and you're not going to be standing here when that stage pulls in. You can scream and carry on, but that's the way it is."

"What about my wife?"

"I can't help her being a woman."

Willard Mims was about to say something, but stopped. His eyes went to the adobe, then back to Usher. He lowered his voice and all the excitement was gone from it. "You know who she is?" He moved closer to Usher. "She's the daughter of old man Gateway, who happens to own part of the third richest copper mine in Arizona. You know what that amounts to? To date, three quarters of a million dollars." He said this slowly, looking straight at Frank Usher.

"Make a point out of it," Usher said.

"Man, it's practically staring you right in the face! You got the daughter of a man who's practically a millionaire. His only daughter! What do you think he'll pay to get her back?"

Frank Usher said, "I don't know. What?"

"Whatever you ask! You sit here waiting for a two-bit holdup and you got a gold mine right in your hands!"

"How do I know she's his daughter?"

Willard Mims looked at Brennan. "You were talking to that driver. Didn't he tell you?"

Brennan hesitated. If the man wanted to bargain with his wife, that was his business. It would give them time; that was the main thing. Brennan nodded. "That's right. His wife is Doretta Gateway."

"Where do you come in?" Usher asked Willard Mims.

"I'm Mr. Gateway's general manager on the Montezuma operation."

Frank Usher was silent now, staring at Mims. Finally he said, "I suppose you'd be willing to ride in with a note."

"Certainly," Mims quickly replied.

"And we'd never see you again."

"Would I save my own skin and leave my wife here?"

Usher nodded. "I believe you would."

"Then there's no use talking about it." Mims shrugged and, watching him, Brennan knew he was acting, taking a long chance.

"We can talk about it," Frank Usher said, "because if we do it, we do it my way." He glanced at the house. "Billy-Jack!" Then to Brennan, "You and him go sit over against the wall."

Billy-Jack came out, and from the wall of the adobe Brennan and Willard watched the three outlaws. They stood in close, and Frank Usher was doing the talking. After a few minutes Billy-Jack went into the adobe again and came out with the yellow stage schedule and an envelope. Usher took them and, against the door of the Concord, wrote something on the back of the schedule.

He came toward them folding the paper into the envelope. He sealed the envelope and handed it with the pencil to Willard Mims. "You put Gateway's name on it and where to find him. Mark it personal and urgent."

Willard Mims said, "I can see him myself and tell him."

"You will," Frank Usher said, "but not how you think. You're going to stop on the main road one mile before you get to Bisbee and give that envelope to somebody passing in. The note tells Gateway you have something to tell him about his daughter and to come alone. When he goes out, you'll tell him the story. If he says no, then he never sees his daughter again. If he says yes, he's to bring fifty thousand in U.S. scrip divided in three saddlebags, to a place up back of the Sasabe. And he brings it alone."

Mims said, "What if there isn't that much cash on hand?"

"That's his problem."

"Well, why can't I go right to his house and tell him?"

"Because Billy-Jack's going to be along to bring you back after you tell him. And I don't want him someplace he can get cornered."

"Oh. . . ."

"That's whether he says yes or no," Frank Usher added.

Mims was silent for a moment. "But how'll Mr. Gateway know where to come?"

"If he agrees, Billy-Jack'll give him directions."

Mims said, "Then when he comes out you'll let us go? Is that it?"

"That's it."

"When do we leave?"

"Right this minute."

"Can I say good-bye to my wife?"

"We'll do it for you."

Brennan watched Billy-Jack come around from the corral, leading two horses. Willard Mims moved toward one of them and they both mounted. Billy-Jack reined his horse suddenly, crowding Mims to turn with him, then slapped Mims's horse on the rump and spurred after it as the horse broke to a run.

Watching them, his eyes half closed, Frank Usher said, "That boy puts his wife up on the stake and then he wants to kiss her good-bye." He glanced at Brennan. "You figure that one for me."

Brennan shook his head. "What I'd like to know is why you only asked for fifty thousand."

Frank Usher shrugged. "I'm not greedy."

★

Chapter Three

Chink turned as the two horses splashed over the creek and grew gradually smaller down the road. He looked at Brennan and then his eyes went to Frank Usher. "We don't have a need for this one, Frank."

Usher's dull eyes flicked toward him. "You bring around the horses and I'll worry about him."

"We might as well do it now as later," Chink said.

"We're taking him with us."

"What for?"

"Because I say so. That reason enough?"

"Frank, we could run him for the well and both take a crack at him."

"Get the horses," Frank Usher said flatly, and stared at Chink until the gunman turned and walked away.

Brennan said, "I'd like to bury this man before we go."

Usher shook his head. "Put him in the well."

"That's no fit place!"

Usher stared at Brennan for a long moment. "Don't push your luck. He goes in the well, whether you do it or Chink does."

Brennan pulled Rintoon's limp body up over his shoulder and carried him across the yard. When he returned, Chink was coming around the adobe with three horses already saddled. Frank Usher stood near the house and now Doretta Mims appeared in the doorway.

Usher looked at her. "You'll have to fork one of these like the rest of us. There ain't no lady's saddle about."

She came out, neither answering nor looking at him.

Usher called to Brennan, "Cut one out of that team and shoot the rest," nodding to the stagecoach.

Minutes later the Sasabe station was deserted.

They followed the creek west for almost an hour before swinging south toward high country. Leaving the creek, Brennan had thought: Five more miles and I'm home. And his eyes hung on the long shallow cup of the Sasabe valley until they entered a trough that climbed winding ahead of them through the hills, and the valley was no longer in view.

Frank Usher led them single file—Doretta Mims, followed by Brennan, and Chink bringing up the rear. Chink rode slouched, swaying with the movement of his dun mare, chewing idly on the drawstring of his hat, and watching Brennan.

Brennan kept his eyes on the woman much of the time. For almost a mile, as they rode along the creek, he had watched her body shaking silently and he knew that she was crying. She had very nearly cried mounting the horse—pulling her skirts down almost desperately, then sitting, holding on to the saddle horn with both hands, biting her lower lip and not looking at them. Chink had sidestepped his dun close to her and said something, and she had turned her head quickly as the color rose from her throat over her face.

They dipped down into a barranca thick with willow and cottonwood and followed another stream that finally disappeared into the rocks at the far end. And after that they began to climb again. For some time they rode through the soft gloom of timber, following switchbacks as the slope became steeper, then came out into the open and crossed a bare gravelly slope, the sandstone peaks above them cold pink in the fading sunlight.

They were nearing the other side of the open grade when Frank Usher said, "Here we are."

Brennan looked beyond him and now he could make out, through the pines they were approaching, a weather-scarred stone-and-log hut built snugly against the steep wall of sandstone. Against one side of the hut was a hide-covered lean-to. He heard Frank Usher say, "Chink, you get the man making a fire and I'll get the woman fixing supper."

There had not been time to eat what the woman had prepared at the stage station and now Frank Usher and Chink ate hungrily, hunkered down a dozen yards out from the lean-to where Brennan and the woman stood.

Brennan took a plate of the jerky and day-old pan bread, but Doretta Mims did not touch the food. She stood next to him, half turned from him, and continued to stare through the trees across the bare slope in the direction they had come. Once Brennan said to her, "You better eat something," but she did not answer him.

When they were finished, Frank Usher ordered them into the hut.

"You stay there the night . . . and if either of you comes near the door, we'll let go, no questions asked. That plain?"

The woman went in hurriedly. When Brennan entered he saw her huddled against the back wall near a corner.

The sod-covered hut was windowless, and he could barely make her out in the dimness. He wanted to go and sit next to her, but it went through his mind that most likely she was as afraid of him as she was of

Frank Usher and Chink. So he made room for himself against the wall where they had placed the saddles, folding a saddle blanket to rest his elbow on as he eased himself to the dirt floor. Let her try and get hold of herself, he thought; then maybe she will want somebody to talk to.

He made a cigarette and lit it, seeing the mask of her face briefly as the match flared, then he eased himself lower until his head was resting against a saddle, and smoked in the dim silence.

Soon the hut was full dark. Now he could not see the woman, though he imagined that he could feel her presence. Outside, Usher and Chink had added wood to the cook fire in front of the lean-to and the warm glow of it illuminated the doorless opening of the hut.

They'll sit by the fire, Brennan thought, and one of them will always be awake. You'd get about one step through that door and *bam*. Maybe Frank would aim low, but Chink would shoot to kill. He became angry thinking of Chink, but there was nothing he could do about it and he drew on the cigarette slowly to make himself relax, thinking: Take it easy: you've got the woman to consider. He thought of her as his responsibility and not even a doubt entered his mind that she was not. She was a woman, alone. The reason was as simple as that.

He heard her move as he was snubbing out the

cigarette. He lay still and he knew that she was coming toward him. She knelt as she reached his side.

"Do you know what they've done with my husband?"

He could picture her drawn face, eyes staring wide open in the darkness. He raised himself slowly and felt her stiffen as he touched her arm. "Sit down here and you'll be more comfortable." He moved over to let her sit on the saddle blanket. "Your husband's all right," he said.

"Where is he?"

"They didn't tell you?"

"No."

Brennan paused. "One of them took him to Bisbee to see your father."

"My father?"

"To ask him to pay to get you back."

"Then my husband's all right." She was relieved, and it was in the sound of her voice.

Brennan said, after a moment, "Why don't you go to sleep now? You can rest back on one of these saddles."

"I'm not tired."

"Well, you will be if you don't get some sleep."

She said then, "They must have known all the time that we were coming."

Brennan said nothing.

"Didn't they?"

"I don't know, ma'am."

"How else would they know about . . . who my father is?"

"Maybe so."

"One of them must have been in Contention and heard my husband charter the coach. Perhaps he had visited Bisbee and knew that my father . . ." Her voice trailed off because she was speaking more to herself than to Brennan.

After a pause Brennan said, "You sound like you feel a little better."

He heard her exhale slowly and he could imagine she was trying to smile.

"Yes, I believe I do now," she replied.

"Your husband will be back sometime tomorrow morning," Brennan said to her.

She touched his arm lightly. "I *do* feel better, Mr. Brennan."

He was surprised that she remembered his name. Rintoon had mentioned it only once, hours before. "I'm glad you do. Now, why don't you try to sleep?"

She eased back gently until she was lying down and for a few minutes there was silence.

"Mr. Brennan?"

"Yes, ma'am."

"I'm terribly sorry about your friend."

"Who?"

"The driver."

"Oh. Thank you."

"I'll remember him in my prayers," she said, and after this she did not speak again.

Brennan smoked another cigarette, then sat unmoving for what he judged to be at least a half hour, until he was sure Doretta Mims was asleep.

Now he crawled across the dirt floor to the opposite wall. He went down on his stomach and edged toward the door, keeping close to the wall. Pressing his face close to the opening, he could see, off to the right side, the fire, dying down now. The shape of a man wrapped in a blanket was lying full length on the other side of it.

Brennan rose slowly, hugging the wall. He inched his head out to see the side of the fire closest to the lean-to, and as he did he heard the unmistakable click of a revolver being cocked. Abruptly he brought his head in and went back to the saddle next to Doretta Mims.

★

Chapter Four

In the morning they brought Doretta Mims out to cook; then sent her back to the hut while they ate. When they had finished they let Brennan and Doretta come out to the lean-to.

Frank Usher said, "That wasn't a head I seen pokin' out the door last night, was it?"

"If it was," Brennan answered, "why didn't you shoot at it?"

"I about did. Lucky thing it disappeared," Usher said. "Whatever it was." And he walked away, through the trees to where the horses were picketed.

Chink sat down on a stump and began making a cigarette.

A few steps from Doretta Mims, Brennan leaned against the hut and began eating. He could see her profile as she turned her head to look out through the trees and across the open slope.

Maybe she *is* a little plain, he thought. Her nose doesn't have the kind of a clean-cut shape that stays in your mind. And her hair—if she didn't have it pulled back so tight she'd look a little younger, and happier. She could do something with her hair. She could do something with her clothes, too, to let you know she's a woman.

He felt sorry for her, seeing her biting her lower lip, still staring off through the trees. And for a reason he did not understand, though he knew it had nothing to do with sympathy, he felt very close to her, as if he had known her for a long time, as if he could look into her eyes—not just now, but anytime—and know what she was thinking. He realized that it was sympathy, in a sense, but not the feeling-sorry kind. He could picture her as a little girl, and self-consciously growing up, and he could imagine vaguely what her father was like. And now—a sensitive girl, afraid of saying the wrong thing; afraid of speaking out of turn even if it meant wondering about instead of knowing what had happened to her husband. Afraid of sounding silly, while men like her husband talked and talked and said nothing. But even having to listen to him, she would not speak against him, because he was her husband.

That's the kind of woman to have, Brennan thought. One that'll stick by you, no matter what. And, he thought, still looking at her, one that's got some insides to her. Not just all on the surface. Probably you would have to lose a woman like that to really appreciate her.

"Mrs. Mims."

She looked at him, her eyes still bearing the anxiety of watching through the trees.

"He'll come, Mrs. Mims. Pretty soon now."

Frank Usher returned and motioned them into the hut again. He talked to Chink for a few minutes and now the gunman walked off through the trees.

Looking out from the doorway of the hut, Brennan said over his shoulder, "One of them's going out now to watch for your husband." He glanced around at Doretta Mims and she answered him with a hesitant smile.

Frank Usher was standing by the lean-to when Chink came back through the trees some time later. He walked out to meet him.

"They coming?"

Chink nodded. "Starting across the slope."

Minutes later two horses came into view crossing the grade. As they came through the trees, Frank Usher called, "Tie up in the shade there!" He and Chink watched the two men dismount, then come across the clearing toward them.

"It's all set!" Willard Mims called.

Frank Usher waited until they reached him. "What'd he say?"

"He said he'd bring the money."

"That right, Billy-Jack?"

Billy-Jack nodded. "That's what he said." He was carrying Rintoon's sawed-off shotgun.

"You didn't suspect any funny business?"

Billy-Jack shook his head.

Usher fingered his beard gently, holding Mims with his gaze. "He can scare up that much money?"

"He said he could, though it will take most of to-day to do it."

"That means he'll come out tomorrow," Usher said.

Willard Mims nodded. "That's right."

Usher's eyes went to Billy-Jack. "You gave him directions?"

"Like you said, right to the mouth of that barranca, chock full of willow. Then one of us brings him in from there."

"You're sure he can find it?"

"I made him say it twice," Billy-Jack said. "Every turn."

Usher looked at Willard Mims again. "How'd he take it?"

"How do you think he took it?"

Usher was silent, staring at Mims. Then he began to stroke his beard again. "I'm asking you," he said.

Mims shrugged. "Of course, he was mad, but there wasn't anything he could do about it. He's a reasonable man."

Billy-Jack was grinning. "Frank, this time tomorrow we're sitting on top of the world."

Willard Mims nodded. "I think you made yourself a pretty good deal."

Frank Usher's eyes had not left Mims. "You want to stay here or go on back?"

"What?"

"You heard what I said."

"You mean you'd let me go . . . now?"

"We don't need you anymore."

Willard Mims's eyes flicked to the hut, then back to Frank Usher. He said, almost too eagerly, "I could go back now and lead old man Gateway out here in the morning."

"Sure you could," Usher said.

"Listen, I'd rather stay with my wife, but if it means getting the old man out here faster, then I think I better go back."

Usher nodded. "I know what you mean."

"You played square with me. By God, I'll play square with you."

Mims started to turn away.

Usher said, "Don't you want to see your wife first?"

Mims hesitated. "Well, the quicker I start traveling, the better. She'll understand."

"We'll see you tomorrow then, huh?"

Mims smiled. "About the same time." He hesitated. "All right to get going now?"

"Sure."

Mims backed away a few steps, still smiling, then turned and started to walk toward the trees. He looked back once and waved.

Frank Usher watched him, his eyes half closed in the sunlight. When Mims was almost to the trees, Usher said, quietly, "Chink, bust him."

Chink fired, the .44 held halfway between waist and shoulders, the long barrel raising slightly as he fired again and again until Mims went down, lying still as the heavy reports faded into dead silence.

★

Chapter Five

Frank Usher waited as Billy-Jack stooped next to Mims. He saw Billy-Jack look up, nodding his head.

"Get rid of him," Usher said, watching now as Billy-Jack dragged Mims's body through the trees to the slope and there let go of it. The lifeless body slid down the grade, raising dust, until it disappeared into the brush far below.

Frank Usher turned and walked back to the hut.

Brennan stepped aside as he reached the low doorway. Usher saw the woman on the floor, her face buried in the crook of her arm resting on one of the saddles, her shoulders moving convulsively as she sobbed.

"What's the matter with her?" he asked.

Brennan said nothing.

"I thought we were doing her a favor," Usher said. He walked over to her, his hand covering the butt of his revolver, and touched her arm with his booted toe. "Woman, don't you realize what you just got out of?"

"She didn't know he did it," Brennan said quietly.

Usher looked at him, momentarily surprised. "No, I don't guess she would, come to think of it." He looked down at Doretta Mims and nudged her again with his boot. "Didn't you know that boy was selling you? This whole idea was his, to save his own skin." Usher paused. "He was ready to leave you again just now . . . when I got awful sick of him way down deep inside."

Doretta Mims was not sobbing now, but still she did not raise her head.

Usher stared down at her. "That was some boy you were married to, would do a thing like that."

Looking from the woman to Frank Usher, Brennan said, almost angrily, "What he did was wrong, but going along with it and then shooting him was all right?"

Usher glanced sharply at Brennan. "If you can't see a difference, I'm not going to explain it to you." He turned and walked out.

Brennan stood looking down at the woman for a few moments, then went over to the door and sat down on the floor just inside it. After a while he could hear Doretta Mims crying again. And for a long time he sat listening to her muffled sobs as he looked out at the sunlit clearing, now and again seeing one of the three outlaws.

He judged it to be about noon when Frank Usher and Billy-Jack rode out, walking their horses across the clearing, then into the trees, with Chink standing looking after them.

They're getting restless, Brennan thought. If they're going to stay here until tomorrow, they've got to be sure nobody's followed their sign. But it would take the best San Carlos tracker to pick up what little sign we made from Sasabe.

He saw Chink walking leisurely back to the lean-to. Chink looked toward the hut and stopped. He stood hip-cocked, with his thumbs in his crossed gun belts.

"How many did that make?" Brennan asked.

"What?" Chink straightened slightly.

Brennan nodded to where Mims had been shot. "This morning."

"That was the seventh," Chink said.

"Were they all like that?" he asked.

"How do you mean?"

"In the back."

"I'll tell you this: Yours will be from the front."

"When?"

"Tomorrow before we leave. You can count on it."

"If your boss gives you the word."

"Don't worry about that," Chink said. Then,

"You could make a run for it right now. It wouldn't be like just standing up gettin' it."

"I'll wait till tomorrow," Brennan said.

Chink shrugged and walked away.

After a few minutes Brennan realized that the hut was quiet. He turned to look at Doretta Mims. She was sitting up, staring at the opposite wall with a dazed expression.

Brennan moved to her side and sat down again. "Mrs. Mims, I'm sorry—"

"Why didn't you tell me it was his plan?"

"It wouldn't have helped anything."

She looked at Brennan now pleadingly. "He could have been doing it for all of us."

Brennan nodded. "Sure he could."

"But you don't believe that, do you?"

Brennan looked at her closely, at her eyes puffed from crying. "Mrs. Mims, you know your husband better than I did."

Her eyes lowered and she said quietly, "I feel very foolish sitting here. Terrible things have happened in these two days, yet all I can think of is myself. All I can do is look at myself and feel very foolish." Her eyes raised to his. "Do you know why, Mr. Brennan? Because I know now that my husband never cared for me; because I know that he married me for his own interest." She paused. "I saw an innocent man killed yesterday and I can't even find the decency within me to pray for him."

"Mrs. Mims, try and rest now."

She shook her head wearily. "I don't care what happens to me."

There was a silence before Brennan said, "When you get done feeling sorry for yourself I'll tell you something."

Her eyes came open and she looked at him, more surprised than hurt.

"Look," Brennan said. "You know it and I know it—your husband married you for your money; but you're alive and he's dead and that makes the difference. You can moon about being a fool till they shoot you tomorrow, or you can start thinking about saving your skin right now. But I'll tell you this—it will take both of us working together to stay alive."

"But he said he'd let us—"

"You think they're going to let us go after your dad brings the money? They've killed four people in less than twenty-four hours!"

"I don't care what happens to me!"

He took her shoulders and turned her toward him. "Well, I care about me, and I'm not going to get shot in the belly tomorrow because you feel sorry for yourself."

"But I can't help!" Doretta pleaded.

"You don't know if you can or not. We've got to keep our eyes open and we've got to think, and when the chance comes we've got to take it quick or else forget about it." His face was close to hers and he was still gripping her shoulders. "These men will kill. They've done it before and they have nothing to lose. They're going to kill us. That means we've got nothing to lose. Now, you think about that a while."

He left her and went back to the door.

Brennan was called out of the hut later in the afternoon, as Usher and Billy-Jack rode in. They had shot a mule deer and Billy-Jack carried a hindquarter dangling from his saddle horn. Brennan was told to dress it down, enough for supper, and the rest to be stripped and hung up to dry.

"But you take care of the supper first," Frank Usher said, adding that the woman wasn't in fit condition for cooking. "I don't want burned meat just 'cause she's in a state over her husband."

After they had eaten, Brennan took meat and coffee in to Doretta Mims.

She looked up as he offered it to her. "I don't care for anything."

He was momentarily angry, but it passed off and he said, "Suit yourself." He placed the cup and plate on the floor and went outside to finish preparing the jerky.

By the time he finished, dusk had settled over the clearing and the inside of the hut was dark as he stepped inside.

He moved to her side and his foot kicked over the tin cup. He stooped quickly, picking up the cup and plate, and even in the dimness he could see that she had eaten most of the food.

"Mr. Brennan, I'm sorry for the way I've acted." She hesitated. "I thought you would understand, else I'd never have told you about—about how I felt."

"It's not a question of my understanding," Brennan said.

"I'm sorry I told you," Doretta Mims said.

He moved closer to her and knelt down, sitting back on his heels. "Look. Maybe I know how you feel, better than you think. But that's not important. Right now you don't need sympathy as much as you need a way to stay alive."

"I can't help the way I feel," she said obstinately.

Brennan was momentarily silent. He said then, "Did you love him?"

"I was married to him!"

"That's not what I asked you. While everybody's being honest, just tell me if you loved him."

She hesitated, looking down at her hands. "I'm not sure."

"But you wanted to be in love with him, more than anything."

Her head nodded slowly. "Yes."

"Did you ever think for a minute that he loved you?"

"That's not a fair question!"

"Answer it anyway!"

She hesitated again. "No, I didn't."

He said, almost brutally, "Then what have you lost outside of a little pride?"

"You don't understand," she said.

"You're afraid you can't get another man—is that what it is? Even if he married you for money, at least he married you. He was the first and last chance as far as you were concerned, so you grabbed him."

"What are you trying to do, strip me of what little self-respect I have left?"

"I'm trying to strip you of this foolishness! You think you're too plain to get a man?"

She bit her lower lip and looked away from him.

"You think nobody'll have you because you bite your lip and can't say more than two words at a time?"

"Mr. Brennan—"

"Listen, you're as much woman as any of them. A hell of a lot more than some, but you've got to realize it! You've got to do something about it!"

"I can't help it if—"

"Shut up with that I-can't-help-it talk! If you can't help it, nobody can. All your life you've been sitting around waiting for something to happen to you. Sometimes you have to walk up and take what you want."

Suddenly he brought her to him, his arms circling her shoulders, and he kissed her, holding his lips to hers until he felt her body relax slowly and at the same time he knew that she was kissing him.

His lips brushed her cheek and he said, close to her, "We're going to stay alive. You're going to do exactly what I say when the time comes, and we're going to get out of here." Her hair brushed his cheek softly and he knew that she was nodding yes.

★

Chapter Six

During the night he opened his eyes and crawled to the lighter silhouette of the doorway. Keeping close to the front wall, he looked out and across to the low-burning fire. One of them, a shadowy form that he could not recognize, sat facing the hut. He did not move, but by the way he was sitting Brennan knew he was awake. You're running out of time, Brennan thought. But there was nothing he could do.

The sun was not yet above the trees when Frank Usher appeared in the doorway. He saw that Brennan was awake and he said, "Bring the woman out," turning away as he said it.

Her eyes were closed, but they opened as Brennan touched her shoulder, and he knew that she had not been asleep. She looked up at him calmly, her features softly shadowed.

"Stay close to me," he said. "Whatever we do, stay close to me."

They went out to the lean-to and Brennan built the fire as Doretta got the coffee and venison ready to put on.

Brennan moved slowly, as if he were tired, as if he had given up hope; but his eyes were alive and most of the time his gaze stayed with the three men—watching them eat, watching them make cigarettes as they squatted in a half circle, talking, but too far away for their voices to be heard. Finally, Chink rose and went off into the trees. He came back with his horse, mounted, and rode off into the trees again but in the other direction, toward the open grade.

It went through Brennan's mind: He's going off like he did yesterday morning, but this time to wait for Gateway. Yesterday on foot, but today on his horse, which means he's going farther down to wait for him. And Frank went somewhere yesterday morning. Frank went over to where the horses are. He suddenly felt an excitement inside of him, deep within his stomach, and he kept his eyes on Frank Usher.

A moment later Usher stood up and started off toward the trees, calling back something to Billy-

Jack about the horses—and Brennan could hardly believe his eyes.

Now. It's now. You know that, don't you? It's now or never. God help me. God help me think of something! And suddenly it was in his mind. It was less than half a chance, but it was something, and it came to him because it was the only thing about Billy-Jack that stood out in his mind, besides the shotgun. *He was always looking at Doretta!*

She was in front of the lean-to, and he moved toward her, turning his back to Billy-Jack sitting with Rintoon's shotgun across his lap.

"Go in the hut and start unbuttoning your dress." He half whispered it and saw her eyes widen as he said it. "Go on! Billy-Jack will come in. Act surprised. Embarrassed. Then smile at him." She hesitated, starting to bite her lip. "Damn it, go on!"

He poured himself a cup of coffee, not looking at her as she walked away. Putting the coffee down, he saw Billy-Jack's eyes following her.

"Want a cup?" Brennan called to him. "There's about one left."

Billy-Jack shook his head and turned the sawed-off shotgun on Brennan as he saw him approaching.

Brennan took a sip of the coffee. "Aren't you going to look in on that?" He nodded toward the hut.

"What do you mean?"

"The woman," Brennan said matter-of-factly. He took another sip of the coffee.

"What about her?" Billy-Jack asked.

Brennan shrugged. "I thought you were taking turns."

"What?"

"Now, look, you can't be so young, I got to draw you a map—" Brennan smiled. "Oh, I see. . . . Frank didn't say anything to you. Or Chink. . . . Keeping her for themselves. . . ."

Billy-Jack's eyes flicked to the hut, then back to Brennan. "They were with her?"

"Well, all I know is Frank went in there yesterday morning and Chink yesterday afternoon while you were gone." He took another sip of the coffee and threw out what was left in the cup. Turning, he said, "No skin off my nose," and walked slowly back to the lean-to.

He began scraping the tin plates, his head down, but watching Billy-Jack. Let it sink through that thick skull of yours. But do it quick! Come on, move, you animal!

There! He watched Billy-Jack walk slowly toward the hut. God, make him move faster! Billy-Jack was out of view then beyond the corner of the hut.

All right. Brennan put down the tin plate he was holding and moved quickly, noiselessly, to the side of the hut and edged along the rough logs until he reached the corner. He listened first before he looked around. Billy-Jack had gone inside.

He wanted to make sure, some way, that Billy-Jack would be looking at Doretta, but there was not time. And then he was moving again—along the front, and suddenly he was inside the hut, seeing the back of Billy-Jack's head, seeing him turning, and a glimpse of Doretta's face, and the sawed-off shotgun coming around. One of his hands shot out to grip the stubby barrel, pushing it, turning it up and back violently, and the other hand closed over the trigger guard before it jerked down on Billy-Jack's wrist.

Deafeningly, a shot exploded, with the twin barrels jammed under the outlaw's jaw. Smoke and a crimson smear, and Brennan was on top of him wrenching the shotgun from squeezed fingers, clutching Billy-Jack's revolver as he came to his feet.

He heard Doretta gasp, still with the ringing in his ears, and he said, "Don't look at him!" already turning to the doorway as he jammed the Colt into his empty holster.

Frank Usher was running across the clearing, his gun in his hand.

Brennan stepped into the doorway leveling the shotgun. "Frank, hold it there!"

Usher stopped dead, but in the next second he was aiming, his revolver coming up even with his face, and Brennan's hand squeezed the second trigger of the shotgun.

Usher screamed and went down, grabbing his knees, and he rolled to his side as he hit the ground. His right hand came up, still holding the Colt.

"Don't do it, Frank!" Brennan had dropped the scattergun and now Billy-Jack's revolver was in his hand. He saw Usher's gun coming in line, and he fired, aiming dead center at the half-reclined figure, hearing the sharp, heavy report, and seeing Usher's gun hand raise straight up into the air as he slumped over on his back.

Brennan hesitated. Get him out of there, quick. Chink's not deaf.

He ran out to Frank Usher and dragged him back to the hut, laying him next to Billy-Jack. He jammed Usher's pistol into his belt. Then, "Come on!" he told Doretta, and took her hand and ran out of the hut and across the clearing toward the side where the horses were.

They moved into the denser pines, where he stopped and pulled her down next to him in the warm sand. Then he rolled over on his stomach and parted the branches to look back out across the clearing.

The hut was to the right. Straight across were more pines, but they were scattered thinly, and through them he could see the sand-colored expanse of the open grade. Chink would come that way, Brennan knew. There was no other way he could.

★

Chapter Seven

Close to him, Doretta said, "We could leave before he comes." She was afraid, and it was in the sound of her voice.

"No," Brennan said. "We'll finish this. When Chink comes we'll finish it once and for all."

"But you don't know! How can you be sure you'll—"

"Listen, I'm not sure of anything, but I know what I have to do." She was silent and he said quietly, "Move back and stay close to the ground."

And as he looked across the clearing his eyes caught the dark speck of movement beyond the trees, out on the open slope. There he was. It had to be him. Brennan could feel the sharp knot in his stomach again as he watched, as the figure grew larger.

Now he was sure. Chink was on foot leading his horse, not coming straight across, but angling higher up on the slope. He'll come in where the trees are thicker, Brennan thought. He'll come out beyond the lean-to and you won't see him until he turns the corner of the hut. That's it. He can't climb the slope back of the hut, so he'll have to come around the front way.

He estimated the distance from where he was lying to the front of the hut—seventy or eighty feet—and his thumb eased back the hammer of the revolver in front of him.

There was a dead silence for perhaps ten minutes before he heard, coming from beyond the hut, "Frank?" Silence again. Then, "Where the hell are you?"

Brennan waited, feeling the smooth, heavy, hickory grip of the Colt in his hand, his finger lightly caressing the trigger. It was in his mind to fire as soon as Chink turned the corner. He was ready. But it came and it went.

It went as he saw Chink suddenly, unexpectedly, slip around the corner of the hut and flatten himself against the wall, his gun pointed toward the door. Brennan's front sight was dead on Chink's belt, but he couldn't pull the trigger. Not like this. He watched Chink edge slowly toward the door.

"Throw it down, boy!"

Chink moved and Brennan squeezed the trigger a split second late. He fired again, hearing the bullet thump solidly into the door frame, but it was too late. Chink was inside.

Brennan let his breath out slowly, relaxing somewhat. Well, that's what you get. You wait, and all you do is make it harder for yourself. He could picture Chink now looking at Usher and Billy-Jack.

That'll give him something to think about. Look at them good. Then look at the door you've got to come out of sooner or later.

I'm glad he's seeing them like that. And he thought then: How long could you stand something like that? He can cover up Billy-Jack and stand it a little longer. But when dark comes. . . . If he holds out till dark he's got a chance. And now he was sorry he had not pulled the trigger before. You got to make him come out, that's all.

"Chink!"

There was no answer.

"Chink, come on out!"

Suddenly gunfire came from the doorway and Brennan, hugging the ground, could hear the swishing of the bullets through the foliage above him.

Don't throw it away, he thought, looking up again. He backed up and moved over a few yards to take up a new position. He'd be on the left side of the doorway as you look at it, Brennan thought, to shoot on an angle like that.

He sighted on the inside edge of the door frame and called, "Chink, come out and get it!" He saw the powder flash, and he fired on top of it, cocked and fired again. Then silence.

Now you don't know, Brennan thought. He reloaded and called out, "Chink!" but there was no answer, and he thought: You just keep digging your hole deeper.

Maybe you did hit him. No, that's what he wants you to think. Walk in the door and you'll find out. He'll wait now. He'll take it slow and start adding up his chances. Wait till night? That's his best bet—but he can't count on his horse being there then. I could have worked around and run it off. And he knows he wouldn't be worth a damn on foot, even if he did get away. So the longer he waits, the less he can count on his horse.

All right, what would you do? Immediately he thought: I'd count shots. So you hear five shots go off in a row and you make a break out the door, and while you're doing it the one shooting picks up another gun. But even picking up another gun takes time.

He studied the distance from the doorway to the corner of the hut. Three long strides. Out of sight in less than three seconds. That's if he's thinking of it. And if he tried it, you'd have only that long to aim and fire. Unless . . .

Unless Doretta pulls off the five shots. He thought about this for some time before he was sure it could be done without endangering her. But first you have to give him the idea.

He rolled to his side to pull Usher's gun from his belt. Then, holding it in his left hand, he emptied it at the doorway. Silence followed.

I'm reloading now, Chink. Get it through your

cat-eyed head. I'm reloading and you've got time to do something.

He explained it to Doretta unhurriedly—how she would wait about ten minutes before firing the first time; she would count to five and fire again, and so on until the gun was empty. She was behind the thick bole of a pine and only the gun would be exposed as she fired.

She said, "And if he doesn't come out?"

"Then we'll think of something else."

Their faces were close. She leaned toward him, closing her eyes, and kissed him softly. "I'll be waiting," she said.

Brennan moved off through the trees, circling wide, well back from the edge of the clearing. He came to the thin section directly across from Doretta's position and went quickly from tree to tree, keeping to the shadows until he was into thicker pines again. He saw Chink's horse off to the left of him. Only a few minutes remained as he came out of the trees to the off side of the lean-to, and there he went down to his knees, keeping his eyes on the corner of the hut.

The first shot rang out and he heard it whump into the front of the hut. One . . . then the second . . . two . . . he was counting them, not moving his eyes from the front edge of the hut . . . three . . . four . . . be ready. . . . Five! Now, Chink!

He heard him—hurried steps on the packed sand—and almost immediately he saw him cutting sharply around the edge of the hut, stopping, leaning against the wall, breathing heavily but thinking he was safe. Then Brennan stood up.

"Here's one facing you, Chink."

He saw the look of surprise, the momentary expression of shock, a full second before Chink's revolver flashed up from his side and Brennan's finger tightened on the trigger. With the report Chink lurched back against the wall, a look of bewilderment still on his face, although he was dead even as he slumped to the ground.

Brennan holstered the revolver and did not look at Chink as he walked past him around to the front of the hut. He suddenly felt tired, but it was the kind of tired feeling you enjoyed, like the bone weariness and sense of accomplishment you felt seeing your last cow punched through the market chute.

He thought of old man Tenvoorde, and only two days ago trying to buy the yearlings from him. He still didn't have any yearlings.

What the hell do you feel so good about?

Still, he couldn't help smiling. Not having money to buy stock seemed like such a little trouble. He saw Doretta come out of the trees and he walked on across the clearing.

6

Jugged

STAN CASS, HIS elbows leaning on the edge of the rolltop desk, glanced over his shoulder as he said, "Take a look how I made this one out."

Marshal John Boynton had just come in. He was standing in the front door of the jail office, one finger absently stroking his full mustache. He looked at his regular deputy, Hanley Miller, who stood next to a chair where a young man sat leaning forward looking at his hands.

"What's the matter with him?" Boynton said, ignoring Stan Cass.

Hanley Miller put his hand on the back of the chair. "A combination of things, John. He's had too many, been beat up, and now he's tired."

"He looks tired," Boynton said, again glancing at the silent young man.

Stan Cass turned his head. "He looks like a smart-aleck kid."

Boynton walked over to Cass and picked up the record book from the desk. The last entry read:

NAME: Pete Given
DESCRIPTION: Nineteen. Medium height and build. Brown hair and eyes. Small scar under chin.
RESIDENCE: Dos Cabezas
OCCUPATION: Mustanger
CHARGE: Drunk and disorderly
COMMENTS: Has to pay a quarter share of the damages in the Continental Saloon whatever they are decided to be.

Boynton handed the record book to Cass. "You spelled *nineteen* wrong."

"Is that all?"

"How do you know he has to pay a quarter of the damages?"

"Being four of them," Cass said mock seriously. "I figured to myself: Now, if they have to chip in for what's busted, how much would—"

"That's for the judge to say. What were they doing here?"

"They delivered a string to the stage line," Cass answered. He was a man in his early twenties, clean shaven, though his sideburns extended down to the curve of his jaw. He was smoking a cigarette and he spoke to Boynton as if he were bored.

"And they tried to spend all the profit in one night," Boynton said.

Cass shrugged indifferently. "I guess so."

Boynton's finger stroked his mustache and he was thinking: Somebody's going to bust his nose for him. He asked, civilly, "Where're the other three?"

Cass nodded to the door that led back to the first-floor cell. "Where else?"

Hanley Miller, the regular night deputy, a man in his late forties, said, "John, you know there's only room for three in there. I was wondering what to do with this boy." He tipped his head toward the quiet young man sitting in the chair.

"He'll have to go upstairs," Boynton said.

"With Obie Ward?"

"I guess he'll have to." Boynton nodded to the boy. "Pull him up."

Hanley Miller got the sleepy boy on his feet.

Cass shook his head watching them. "Obie Ward's got everybody buffaloed. I'll be a son of a gun if he ain't got everybody buffaloed."

Boynton's eyes dropped to Cass, but he did not say anything.

"I'm just saying that Obie Ward don't look so tough," Cass said.

"Act like you've got some sense once in a while," Boynton said now. He had hired Cass the week before as an extra night guard—the day they brought in Obie Ward—but he was certain now he would not keep Cass. Tomorrow he would look around for somebody else. Somebody who didn't talk so much and didn't have such a proud opinion of himself.

"All I'm saying is he don't look so tough to me," Cass repeated.

Boynton ignored him. He looked at the young man, Pete Given, standing next to Hanley now with his eyes closed, and he heard his deputy say, "The boy's asleep on his feet."

"He looks familiar," Boynton said.

"We had him here about three months ago."

"Same thing?"

Hanley nodded. "Delivered his horses, then stopped off at the Continental. Remember, his wife come here looking for him. He was here five days because the judge was away and she got here court day. Pretty little thing with light-colored hair? Not more'n seventeen. Come all the way from Dos Cabezas by herself."

"Least he had sense enough to get a good woman," Boynton said. He seemed to hesitate. Then: "You and I'll take him up." He slipped his revolver from its holster and placed it on the desk. He took young Pete Given's arm then and raised it up over his shoulder, glancing at his deputy again. "Hanley, you come behind with your shotgun."

Cass watched them go through the door and down the hall to the back of the jail to the outside stairway, and he was thinking: Won't even wear his gun up there, he's so scared. That's some man to work for, won't even wear his gun when he goes in Ward's cell. He shook his head and said the name again, contemptuously. Obie Ward. He'd pull his tough act on me just once.

★ ★ ★

PETE GIVEN OPENED his eyes. Lying on his right side his face was close to the wall and for a moment, seeing the chipped and peeling adobe and smelling the stale mildewed smell of the mattress which did not have a cover on it, he did not know where he was. Then he remembered, and he closed his eyes again.

The sour taste of whiskey coated his mouth and he lay very still, waiting for the throbbing to start in his head. But it did not come. He raised his head and moved closer to the wall and felt the edge of the mattress cool and firm against his cheek. Still the throbbing did not come. There was a dull tight feeling at the base of his skull, but not the shooting sharp pain he had expected. That was good. He moved his toes and could feel his boots still on and there was no blanket covering him.

They just dumped you here, he thought. He made saliva in his mouth and kept swallowing until his mouth did not feel sticky and some of the sour taste went away. Well, what did you expect?

It's about all you deserve, buddy. No, it's more'n you deserve.

You'll learn, huh?

He thought of his wife, Mary Ellen, and his eyes closed tighter and for a moment he tried not to think of anything.

How do I do this? How do I get something good, then kick it away like it's not worth anything?

What'll you tell her this time?

"Mary Ellen, honest to gosh, we just went in to get one drink. We sold the horses and got something to eat and figured one drink before starting back. Then Art said one more. All right, just one, I told him. But, you know, we were relaxed—and laughing. That's hard work running a thirty-horse string for five days. Harry got in a blackjack game. The rest of us were just sitting relaxed. When you're sitting like that the time seems to go faster. We had a few drinks. Maybe four—five at the most. Like I said, we were laughing and Art was telling some stories. You know Art, he keeps talking—then there's a commotion over at the blackjack table and we see Harry haulin' off at this man. And—"

And Mary Ellen will say, "Just like the last time," not raising her voice or seeming mad, but she'll keep looking you right in the eye.

"Honey, those things just happen. I can't help it. And it wasn't just like last time."

"The result's the same," she'll say. "You work hard for three months to earn decent money then pay it all out in fines and damages."

"Not all of it."

"It might as well be all. We can't live on what's left."

"But I can't help it. Can't you see that? Harry got in a fight and we had to help him. It's just one of those things that happens. You can't help it."

"But it seems a little silly, doesn't it?"

"Mary Ellen, you don't understand."

"Doesn't throwing away three months' profit in one night seem silly to you?"

"You don't understand."

You can be married to a girl for almost a year and think you know her and you don't know her at all. That's it. You know how she talks, but you don't know what she's thinking. That's a big difference. But there's some things you can't explain to a woman anyway.

He felt a little better. Facing her would not be pleasant—but it still wasn't his fault.

He rolled over, momentarily studying the ceiling, then he let his head roll on the mattress and he saw the man on the other bunk watching him. He was sitting hunched over, making a cigarette.

Pete Given closed his eyes and he could still see the man. He didn't seem big, but he had a stringy hard-boned look. Sharp cheekbones and dull-black hair that was cut short and brushed forward to his forehead. No mustache, but he needed a shave and it gave the appearance of an almost full-grown mustache.

He opened his eyes again. The man was drawing on the cigarette, still watching him.

"What time you think it is?" Given asked.

"About nine." The man's voice was clear though he barely moved his mouth.

Given said, "If you were one of them over to the Continental I'd just as soon shake hands this morning."

The man did not reply.

"You weren't there, then?"

"No," he said now.

"What've they got you for?"

"They say I shot a man."

"Oh."

"Fact is, they say I shot two men, during the Grant stage holdup."

"Oh."

"When the judge comes tomorrow, he'll set a court date. Give the witnesses time to get here." He stood up, saying this. He was tall, above average, but not heavy.

"Are you"—Given hesitated—"Obie Ward?"

The man nodded, drawing on the cigarette.

"Somebody last night said you were here. I'd forgot about it." Given spoke louder, trying to make his voice sound natural, and now he raised himself on an elbow.

Obie Ward asked, "Were you drinking last night?"

"Some."

"And got in a fight."

Given sat up, swinging his legs off the bunk and resting his elbows on his knees. "One of my partners got in trouble and we had to help him."

"You don't look so good," Ward said.

"I feel okay."

"No," Ward said. "You don't look so good."

"Well, maybe I just look worse'n I am."

"How's your stomach?"

"It's all right."

"You look sick to me."

"I could eat. Outside of that I got no complaint." Given stood up. He put his hands on the small of his back and stretched, feeling the stiffness in his body. Then he raised his arms straight up, stretching again, and yawned. That felt good. He saw Obie Ward coming toward him, and he lowered his arms.

Ward reached out, extending one finger, and poked it at Pete Given's stomach. "How's it feel right there?"

"Honest to gosh, it feels okay." He smiled looking at Ward, to show that he was willing to go along with a joke, but he felt suddenly uneasy. Ward was standing too close to him and Given was thinking: What's the matter with him?—and the same moment he saw the beard-stubbled face tighten.

Ward went back a half step and came forward, driving his left fist into Given's stomach. The boy started to fold, a gasp coming from his open mouth, and Ward followed with his right hand, bringing it up solidly against the boy's jaw, sending him back, arms flung wide, over the bunk and hard against the wall. Given slumped on the mattress and did not move. For a moment Ward looked at him, then picked up his cigarette from the floor and went back to his bunk.

He was sitting on the edge of it when Given opened his eyes—smoking another cigarette, drawing on it and blowing the smoke out slowly.

"Are you sick now?"

Given moved his head, trying to lift it, and it was an effort to do this. "I think I am."

Ward started to rise. "Let's make sure."

"I'm sure."

☆ ☆ ☆

WARD RELAXED AGAIN. "I told you so, but you didn't believe me. I been watching you all morning and the more I watched, the more I thought to myself: Now there's a sick boy. Maybe you ought to even have a doctor."

Given said nothing. He stiffened as Ward rose and came toward him.

"What's the matter? I'm just going to see you're more comfortable." Ward leaned over, lifting the boy's legs one at a time, and pulled his boots off, then pushed him, gently, flat on the bunk and covered him with a blanket that was folded at the foot of it. Given looked up, holding his body rigid, and saw Ward shake his head. "You're a mighty sick boy. We got to do something about that."

Ward crossed the cell to his bunk, and standing at one end, he lifted it a foot off the floor and let it drop. He did this three times, then went down to his hands and knees and, close to the floor, called, "Hey, Marshal!" He waited. "Marshal, we got a sick boy up here!" He rose, winking at Given, and sat down on his bunk.

Minutes later a door at the back end of the hallway opened and Boynton came toward the cell. A deputy with a shotgun, his day man, followed him.

"What's the matter?"

Ward nodded. "The boy's sick."

"He ought to be," Boynton said.

Ward shrugged. "Don't matter to me, but I got to listen to him moaning."

Boynton looked toward Given's bunk. "A man that don't know how to drink has got to expect that." He turned abruptly. Their steps moved down the hall and the door slammed closed.

"No sympathy," Ward said. He made another cigarette, and when he had lit it he walked over to Given's bunk. "He'll come back in about two hours with our dinner. You'll still be in bed, and this time you'll be moaning like you got belly cramps. You got that?"

Staring up at him, Given nodded his head stiffly.

At a quarter to twelve Boynton came up again. This time he ordered Ward to lie down flat on his bunk. He unlocked the door then and remained in the hall as the day man came in with the dinner tray and placed it in the middle of the floor.

"He still sick?" Boynton stood in the doorway holding a sawed-off shotgun.

Ward turned his head on the mattress. "Can't you hear him?"

"He'll get over it."

"I think it's something else," Ward said. "I never saw whiskey hold on like that."

"You a doctor?"

"As much a one as you are."

Boynton looked toward the boy again. Given's eyes were closed and he was moaning faintly. "Tell him to eat something," Boynton said. "Maybe then he'll feel better."

"I'll do that," Ward said. He was smiling as Boynton and his deputy moved off down the hall.

Lying on his back, his head turned on the mattress, Given watched Ward take a plate from the tray. It looked like stew.

"Can I have some?" Given said.

Chewing, Ward shook his head.

"Why not?"

Ward swallowed. "You're too sick."

"Can I ask you a question?"

"Go ahead."

"How come I'm sick?"

"You haven't figured it?"

"No."

"I'll give you a hint. We'll get our supper about six. Watch the two that bring it up."

"I don't see what they'd have to do with me."

"You don't have to see."

Given was silent for some time. He said then, "It's got to do with you busting out."

Obie Ward grinned. "You got a head on your shoulders."

Boynton came up a half hour later. He stood in the hall and when his deputy brought out the tray, his eyes went from it to Pete Given's bunk. "The boy didn't eat a bite," Boynton observed.

Ward raised up on his elbow. "Said he couldn't stand the smell of it." He watched Boynton look toward the boy, then sank down on the bunk again as Boynton walked away. When the door down the hall closed, Ward said, "Now he believes it."

It was quiet in the cell after that. Ward rolled over to face the wall and Pete Given, lying on his back, remained motionless, though his eyes were open and he was studying the ceiling.

He tried to understand Obie Ward's plan. He tried to see how his being sick could have anything to do with Ward's breaking out. And he thought: He means what he says, doesn't he? You can be sure of that much. He's going to bust out and you got a part in it and there ain't a damn thing you can do about it. It's that simple, isn't it?

★ ★ ☆

OBIE WARD WAS RIGHT. At what seemed close to six o'clock they heard the door open at the end of the hall and a moment later Stan Cass and Hanley Miller were standing in front of the cell. Hanley opened the door and stood holding a sawed-off shotgun as Cass came in with the tray.

Cass half turned to face Ward sitting on his bunk, then went down to one knee, lowering the tray to the floor, and he did not take his eyes from Ward. He rose then and turned as he heard groans from the other bunk.

"What's his trouble?"

Ward looked up. "Didn't your boss tell you?"

"He told me," Cass said, "but I believe what I see."

"Help yourself, then."

Cass turned sharply. "You shut your mouth till I want to hear from you!"

"Yes, sir," Ward said. His dark face was expressionless.

Cass stared at him, his thumbs hooked in his gun belt. "You think you're somethin', don't you?"

Ward's head moved from side to side. "Not me."

"I'd like to see you pull somethin'," Cass said.

His right hand opened and closed, moving closer to his hip. "I'd just like to see you get off that bunk and pull somethin'."

Ward shook his head. "Somebody's been telling you stories."

"I think they have," Cass said. He hesitated, then walked out, slamming the door shut.

Ward called to him through the bars, "What about the boy?"

"You take care of him," Cass said, moving off. Hanley Miller followed, looking back over his shoulder.

Ward waited until the back door closed, then picked up a plate and began to eat and not until he was almost finished did he notice Given watching him.

"Did you see anything?"

Given came up on his elbow slowly. He looked at the tray on the floor, then at Ward. "Like what?"

"Like the way that deputy acted."

"He wanted you to try something."

"What else?"

Given pictured Cass again in his mind. "He was wearing a gun." Suddenly he seemed to understand and he said, "The marshal wasn't wearing any, but this one was!"

Ward grinned. "And he knows you're sick. First his boss told him, then he saw it with his own eyes." Ward put down the plate and he made a cigarette as he walked over to Given's bunk. "I'll tell you something else," he said, standing close to the bunk. "I've been here seven days. For seven days I watch. I see the marshal. He knows what he's doing and he don't wear a gun when he comes in here. A man out in the hall with a scattergun's enough. Then this other one they call Cass. He walks like he can feel his gun on his hip. He's not used to it, but it feels good and he'd like an excuse to use it. He even wears it in here, though likely he's been told not to. What does that tell you? He's sure of himself, but he's not smart. He wants to see me try something—and he's sure he can get his gun out if I do. For seven days I see this and there's nothing I can do about it—until this morning."

Given nodded thoughtfully, but said nothing.

"This morning I saw you," Ward went on, "and you looked sick. There it was."

Given nodded again. "I guess I see."

"We let the marshal know about it. He tells Cass when he comes on duty. Cass comes up and sure enough, you're sick."

"Yeah?"

"Then Cass comes up the next time—understand it'll be dark outside by then: he brings supper up at six, but he must go out to eat after that because he doesn't come back for the tray till almost eight—and he's not surprised to see you even sicker."

"How does he see that?"

"You scream like your stomach's been pulled out and you roll off the bunk."

"Then what?"

"Then you don't have to do anything else."

Given's eyes held on Ward's face. He swallowed and said, as evenly as he could, "Why should I help you escape?" He saw it coming and he tried to roll away, but it was too late and Ward's fist came down against his face like a mallet.

He was dazed and there was a stinging throbbing over the entire side of his face, but he was conscious of Ward leaning close to him and he heard the words clearly. "I'll kill you. That reason enough?"

After that he was not conscious of time. His eyes were closed and for a while he dozed off. Then, when he opened his eyes, momentarily he could remember nothing and he was not even sure where he was, because he was thinking of nothing, only looking at the chipped and peeling adobe wall and feeling a strange numbness over the side of his face.

His hand was close to his face and his fingers moved to touch his cheekbone. The skin felt swollen hard and tight over the bone, and just touching it was painful. He thought then: Are you afraid for your own neck? Of course I am!

But it was more than fear that was making his heart beat faster. There was an anger inside of him. Anger adding excitement to the fear and he realized this, though not coolly, for he was thinking of Ward and Mary Ellen and himself as they came into his mind, not as he called them there.

Ward had said, Roll off the cot.

All right.

He heard the back door open and instantly Ward muttered, "You awake?" He turned his head to see Ward sitting on the edge of the bunk, his hands at his sides gripping the mattress. He heard the footsteps coming up the hall.

"I'm awake."

"Soon as he opens the door," Ward said, and his shoulders seemed to relax.

As soon as he opens the door.

He heard Cass saying something and a key rattled in the lock. The squeak of the door hinges—

He groaned, bringing his knees up. His heart was pounding and a heat was over his face and he kept his eyes squeezed closed. He groaned again, louder this time, and doing it he rolled to his side, hesitated at the edge of the mattress, then let himself fall heavily to the floor.

"What's the matter with him!"

Four steps on the plank floor vibrated in his ear.

A hand took his shoulder and rolled him over. Opening his eyes, he saw Cass leaning over him.

Suddenly then, Cass started to rise, his eyes stretched open wide, and he twisted his body to turn. An arm came from behind hooking his throat, dragging him back, and a hand was jerking the revolver from its holster.

* * *

HANLEY MILLER tried to push away from the bars to bring up the shotgun. It clattered against the bars and on top of the sound came the deafening report of the revolver. Hanley doubled up and went to the floor, clutching his thigh.

Cass's mouth was open and he was trying to scream as the revolver flashed over his head and came down. The next moment Ward was throwing Cass's limp weight aside. Ward stumbled, clattering over the tray in the middle of the floor, almost tripping.

Given saw Ward go through the wide-open door. He glanced then at Hanley Miller lying on the floor. Then, looking at Ward's back, the thought stabbed suddenly, unexpectedly, in his mind—

Get him!

He hesitated, though the hesitation was in his mind and it was part of a moment. Then he was on his feet, moving quickly, silently, in his stocking feet, stooping to pick up the sawed-off shotgun, turning and seeing Ward near the door. Now Given was running down the hallway, now swinging open the door that had just closed behind Ward.

Ward was on the back-porch landing, starting down the stairs, and he wheeled, bringing up the revolver as the door opened, as he saw Pete Given on the landing, as he saw the stubby shotgun barrels swinging savagely in the dimness.

Ward fired hurriedly, wildly, the same moment the double barrels slashed against the side of his head. He screamed as he lost his balance and went down the stairway. At the bottom he tried to rise, groping momentarily, feverishly, for his gun. As he came to his feet, Pete Given was there—and again the shotgun cut viciously against his head. Ward went down, falling forward, and this time he did not move.

Given sat down on the bottom step, letting the shotgun slip from his fingers. A lantern was coming down the alley.

Boynton appeared in the circle of lantern light. He looked from Obie Ward to the boy, not speaking, but his eyes remained on Given until he stepped past him and went up the stairs.

A man stooped next to him, extending an already rolled cigarette. "You look like you want a smoke."

Given shook his head. "I'd swallow it."

The man nodded toward Obie Ward. "You took him by yourself?"

"Yes, sir."

"That must've been something to see."

"I don't know—it happened so fast." In the crowd he heard Obie Ward's name over and over—someone asking if he was dead, a man bending over him saying no . . . someone asking, "Who's that boy?" and someone answering, "I don't know, but he's got enough guts for everybody."

Boynton appeared on the landing and called for someone to get the doctor. He came down and Given stood up to let him pass. The man who was holding the cigarette said, "John, this boy got Obie all by himself."

Boynton was looking at Ward. "I see that."

"More'n I would've done," the man said, shaking his head.

"More'n most anybody would've done," Boynton answered. He looked at Given then, studying him openly. He said then, "I'll recommend to the judge we drop the charges against you."

Given nodded. "That'd be fine."

"Anxious to get home to your wife?"

"Yes, sir."

For a moment Boynton was silent. His expression was mild, but his eyes were fastened on Pete Given's face as if he were trying to read something there, some mark of character that would tell him about this boy.

"On second thought," Boynton said abruptly, "I'll tear your name right out of the record book, if you'll take a deputy job. You won't even have to put a foot in court."

Given looked up. "You mean that?"

"I got two jobs open," Boynton said. He hesitated before adding, "Look, it's up to you. Probably I'll tear your name out even if you don't take the job. Seeing the condition of Obie Ward, I wouldn't judge you're a man who's going to be pressured into anything."

Given's face showed surprise, but it was momentary, his mouth relaxing into a slow grin—almost as if the smile widened as Boynton's words sank into his mind—and he said, "I'll have to go to Dos Cabezas and get my wife."

Boynton nodded. "Will she be happy about this?"

Pete Given was still smiling. "Marshal, you and I probably couldn't realize how happy she'll be."

7

The Kid

I REMEMBER LOOKING out the window, hearing the wagon, and saying to Terry McNeil and Delia, "Here comes Repper." And when the wagon came even with the porch, I saw the boy. He was sitting with his legs hanging over the end-gate, but he came forward when Max Repper motioned to him.

That was the first time any of us laid eyes on the boy, and I'll tell you frankly we weren't positive at first it was a boy, even though Max Repper referred to a "him," saying, "Don't let his long hair fool you," and even though up close we could see the features didn't belong to a girl. Still, with the extent of my travel bounded by the Mogollon Rim country, central Sonora, the Pecos River, and the Kofa Mountains—north, south, east, and west respectively—I wasn't going to confine my judgment to this being either just a boy or a girl. There are many things in the world I haven't seen, and the way Terry McNeil was keeping his mouth closed I suspect he was reserving judgment on the same grounds.

Terry was in to buy stores for his prospecting site in the Dragoons. He came in usually about every two weeks, but by the little bit he'd buy it was plain he came for Delia more than for flour and salt-meat.

It was just the three of us in the store when Max Repper came—Terry, taking his time like he was planning to outfit an expedition; Deelie, my girl-child, helping him and hoping he'd take all day; and me. Me being the first line of the sign outside that says PATTERSON GENERAL SUPPLIES. BANDERAS, ARIZONA, TERR.

Now, this Max Repper was a man who saddle-tamed horses on a little place he had a few miles up the creek. He sold them to anybody who needed a horse; sometimes a few to the Cavalry Station at Dos Fuegos, though most often their remounts were all matched and came down from Whipple

Barracks. So Max Repper sold mainly to the one hundred and eighty-odd souls who lived in and around Banderas.

He also operated a livery here in the settlement, but even Max admitted it wasn't a paying proposition and ordinarily he wasn't one to come right out and say he was holding a bad guess. Max was a hard-nosed individual, like a man had to be to mustang for a living; but he also had a mile-high opinion of himself, and if any living creature sympathized with him it'd have to have been one of his horse string. Though the way Max broke a horse, the possibility of that was even doubtful.

Repper came in with the boy behind him and he said to me, "Pat, look what the hell I found."

I asked him, "What is it?"

And he said, "Don't let the long hair fool you. It's a boy . . . a *white* boy."

We had to take Max's word for it at first, for that boy cut the strangest figure I ever saw. Maybe twelve years old, he was, with long dark hair hanging to his shoulders Apache style, matted and tangled, but he didn't have on a rag headband and that's why you didn't think of Apache when you looked at him, even though his skin was weathered mahogany and the rest of his getup might have been Indian. His shirt was worn-out cotton and open all the way down, no buttons left; his pants were buckskin, homemade by Indian or Mexican, you couldn't tell which, and he wasn't wearing shoes.

The bare feet made you feel sorry for him even after you looked close and saw something half wild about him. You wondered if the mind was translating what the eyes saw into man-talk or into some kind of gray-shadowed animal understanding.

★ ★ ★

TERRY MCNEIL WAS toward the back, leaning on the counter close to Delia. They were just looking. I got up from the desk (it was by the front window and served as "office" for the Hatch & Hodges Line's Banderas station), but I just stood there, not wanting to go up and gawk at the boy like he was P. T. Barnum's ten-cent attraction.

"The good are rewarded," Max Repper said. He grinned showing his crooked yellow teeth, which always took the humor out of anything funny he ever said. "I was thinking about hiring a boy when I found this one." He looked at the boy standing motionless. "He's going to work for me free."

I asked now, "Where'd you find him?"

"Snoopin' around my stores."

"Where's he from?"

"Damn' if I know. He don't even talk."

Max pulled the boy forward by the shoulder right up in front of me and said, "What do you judge his breed to be?" Like the boy was a paint mustang with spots Max hadn't ever seen before.

I asked him again where he'd found the boy and he told how a few nights ago he'd heard something in the lean-to back of his shack, and had eased out there in his sock feet and jabbed a Henry in the boy's back as he was taking down Max's fresh jerky strings.

He kept the boy tied up the rest of the night and fed him in the morning, watched him stuff jerked venison into his mouth, asked him where he came from, and got only grunts for answers.

He put the boy to work watering his corral mounts, and the way the boy roughed the horses told Max maybe there was Apache in his background. But Max didn't know any Apache words and the boy wasn't volunteering any. Max thought of Spanish. The only trouble was he didn't know Spanish either.

The second night the boy tried to run away and Max (grinning as he told it) beat him blue. The third morning Max decided (reluctantly) he'd have to bring the boy in for shoeing. Shoes cost money, but barefooted a boy don't work so good—not on a south Arizona horse ranch.

I realized then Max was honest-to-goodness

planning on keeping the boy, but I mentioned, just to make sure, "I suppose you'll take him to Dos Fuegos and turn him over to the Army."

"What for? He don't belong to them."

"He don't belong to you either."

"He sure as hell does. Long as I feed him."

I told Max, "Maybe the Army can trace where this boy came from."

But Repper said he'd tried for two days to get something out of the boy, and if he couldn't, then no lousy Army man could expect to.

"The kid's had his chance to talk," Max said. "If he don't want to, all right, then. I'll draw him pictures of what to do and push him to'ard it."

Max sat the boy down on a stool and I handed the shoes to him and he jammed them on the boy's feet until he thought he'd found the right size. When Max started to button one of them up the boy yanked his foot away and grunted like it hurt him. Max reached up and swatted the boy across the face and he kept still then.

I remember thinking: He handles the boy like he would a wild mustang, not like a human being. And Terry McNeil must have been thinking the same thing. He came up to us, then knelt down next to the boy, ignoring Max Repper, who was ready to put on the other shoe.

The boy looked at Terry and seemed to back off,

maybe just a couple of inches on the outside, but the way he tensed you knew an iron door slammed shut inside of him.

Max said, "What in the name of George H. Hell you think you're doing?" Max had no use for Terry—but I'll tell you about that later.

Terry looked up at Repper and said, "I thought I'd just talk to him."

Max most probably wanted to kick Terry in the teeth, especially now, worn out from trying on shoes, and on general principle besides. Terry was the kind of boy who never let anything bother him, never raised his voice, and I know for a fact that burned Max, especially when they had differences of opinion, which was about every other time they ran into each other.

Max was near the end of his short-sized temper, but he held on and forced out a laugh to show Terry what he thought of him and said to me, "Pat, I'm going to buy myself a drink."

I kept just a couple of bottles for customers who didn't have time to get down to the State House. Serving Max, I watched Terry and the boy.

★ ★ ★

TERRY WAS SITTING cross-legged in front of him now slipping off the shoe Max had buttoned up.

He took another from the pile of shoes and tried it on, the boy letting him, watching curiously, and I could hear Terry saying something in that slow, quiet way he talked. First, I thought it was Spanish, and maybe it was, but the little bit I could hear after that was a low mumble . . . then bit-off crisp words like *sik-isn* and *nakai*-yes and *pesh-klitso,* though not used together. The kind of talk you hear up at the San Carlos Reservation.

Then Terry leaned close to the boy and for a while I couldn't see the boy's face. Terry leaned back and said something else; then he touched the boy's arm, holding it for a moment, and when he stood up the boy's eyes followed him and they no longer had that locked iron door behind them.

Terry came over to us and said, "The boy was taken from the Mexican village of Sahuaripa something like three years ago. He was out watching the men herd cattle when a Chiricahua raiding party hit them. They killed the others and carried off the boy."

Max didn't speak, so I said, "I thought he was white."

Terry nodded his head. "His Mexican father told him that his real parents had died when he was a small boy. The Mexican had hired out to them as a guide, but they both died of a fever on the way to wherever they were going. So the Mexican went home to Sahuaripa and took the boy with him. He explained to the boy that he and his wife had never had a child, but they had prayed, and he believed the boy to be God's answer. They named the boy Regalo."

Max said, "You expect me to believe that?"

Terry shrugged. "Why shouldn't you?"

Max just looked at Terry, then grinned and shook his head slowly like saying: You think I was born last week? Terry might have told him what he thought, but Repper stomped out, dragging the boy and his new shoes with him.

I said to Terry, "The boy really tell you that?"

"Sure he did."

"What about the past three years?"

"He's been with Chiricahuas. Made blood son of Juh, who's chief of the whole red she-bang." Terry said the boy had wandered off on a lone hunt; his horse lamed and he was cutting back home when he came across Max's place.

"Terry," I said, "I imagine a boy could learn a lot of mean things from Chiricahuas."

And Terry said, "That's why I'm almost tempted to feel sorry for old Max."

Terry went back to outfitting for his expedition, but now he actually put his list down and asked Deelie to fill it. He didn't stay more than ten minutes after that, talking to Deelie, telling her what

the boy said. And when he was gone I asked Deelie
what his big hurry was.

"I never saw a man so eager to get back to a mine
camp," I said.

"Terry's anxious to make this one pay," Deelie
said. There was a soft smile on her face and she
dropped her eyes quick, which was Deelie's way of
telling you she had a secret—though I suspected it
was something more akin to wishful thinking.
Terry McNeil was never too anxious about anything.

He took everything in long, easy strides, even
pretty little seventeen-year-old things like Deelie. I
know he was taken with her, ever since the first day
he set foot here, which was two years ago. He came
through on his way to Dos Fuegos, riding dispatch
for General Stoneman, and stopped off to buy a
pound of Arbuckle's (he said that ration coffee put
him to sleep); Deelie waited on him and I remember
he looked at her like she was the only woman between Whipple Barracks and the border. Deelie ate
it up and stood by the window after he was gone.
Three weeks later he showed up again with a
shovel, a pick, and boards for a sluice box; and said
he'd once seen a likely placer up in the Dragoons
and he'd always wanted to test it and now he was
going to.

He must have saved his dispatch-riding money,

because the first year and a half he paid his store bill cash and carry though he never struck anything likelier than quartz. Lately, he hadn't been buying so much.

★ ★ ★

I NEVER HAVE disrespected him for not wanting to work steady. That's his business. Max Repper called him a saddle tramp—not to his face—but whenever he referred to Terry. You see, the big war between those two started over Deelie. Max thought he had priority, even though Deelie practically told him right out she didn't care for him. Then Terry came along and Deelie about strained her back putting on extra charm. Max saw this and blamed Terry for stealing her affections. Max himself, being close to pushing forty and with those yellow snag teeth, couldn't have stole her affections with seven hundred Henry rifles.

Maybe Deelie and Terry were closer now than when they first met, but I didn't judge so close as to make Terry *run* back to his diggings to work on the marriage stake. Right after he left, it dawned on me that he would have to pass Repper's place on the way. So that was probably why he left on the run: to look in there. Repper was burning when he left, and a man of his sour nature was likely to take out his anger even on a boy.

Terry came back about three weeks later. He tied his horse, stood on the porch, and took time to stretch the saddle kinks out of his back while Deelie waited behind the counter dying. And when he came in she gave him a smile brighter than the sun flash of a U.S. Army heliograph. Deelie's smile would come right up from her toes.

"Terry!"

He gave her a nice smile.

I told him, "You look happy enough, but not like you're ready to celebrate pay dirt."

"Getting warmer, Mr. Patterson," he said. Which is what he always said.

"Have you seen the boy?" I asked. And was a little surprised when he nodded right away.

"Saw him this morning."

"How so?"

"Well," Terry said, "I was over to Dos Fuegos last week, and you know that big black-haired lieutenant, the married one with the little boy?" I nodded. "He sold me one of his son's shirts. A red one from St. Louis."

"And you gave it to the boy."

Terry nodded. "Regalo."

"You rode all the way over to Dos Fuegos to buy a shirt for the boy."

"A red one—"

"From St. Louis. How'd he like it?"

"He liked it fine."

"How'd Repper like it?"

"He was in the shack."

Terry asked me if I'd seen the boy and I told him no. Repper had kept to his horse camp since the first time he brought the boy in. Terry said the boy looked all right in body, but not in his eyes.

* * *

LATER ON, AFTER I'd closed up, the three of us were sitting in back having something to eat—Deelie showing off what a good cook she was—when I heard someone at the front door.

Everyone in Banderas knows what time I close; still, it could have been something special, so I walked up front through the dark store and opened the door.

Maybe you've guessed it. I sure didn't. It was the boy, Regalo. He just stood there and I had to take him by the arm and bring him inside. Then, when we reached the light, I saw what was the matter.

He had on the red shirt but the back of it was almost in shreds, and crisscrossing his bare skin were raw welts, ugly red-looking burns like a length of manila had been sanded across his back a couple of dozen times.

Terry was up out of the chair and we eased the
boy into it and made him lean forward over the
table. Terry knelt down close to him and started to
talk in Spanish. Ordinarily I know some, but not
the way Terry was running the words together.
Then the boy spoke. While he did, Deelie went out
and came back with some cocoa butter and she
spread it over his back gently without batting an
eye. I think right then she advanced seven hundred
feet in Terry McNeil's estimation.

The boy said, Terry told us, that Repper had
come out of the house and when he saw the new
shirt he tried to rip it off the boy, but Regalo ran.
That made Repper mad and when he caught him at
the barn he reached a hackamore line off a nail and
laid it across the boy's back until his arm got tired.

Leaning over the table, the boy didn't cry or
whimper, but you knew his back stung like fire.

Terry was saying, let's fix him some eggs, when
we heard the door again . . . then heavy footsteps
and there was Max Repper in the doorway with his
Henry rifle square on us.

"The boy's coming with me." That's all he said.
He took Regalo by the arm, yanked him out of the
chair, marched him through the front part, and out
the door. It happened so fast, I hardly realized Max
had been there.

Terry was in the doorway looking up toward the

front door. He didn't say a word. Probably he was thinking he should have done something, even if it had happened fast and Max was holding a Henry. Whatever he was thinking, he made up his mind fast. Terry took one last glance at Deelie and was gone.

Of course we knew where he was going. First to the boardinghouse for his gun, then to the livery, then to Repper's place. We didn't want him to do it . . . but at the same time, we did. The only thing was, someone else should be there. I figured whatever was going to happen ought to have a witness. So I saddled up and rode out about fifteen minutes behind Terry.

I thought I might catch him on the road, but didn't see a soul and finally I cut off to Repper's. There was Terry's claybank and just over the rump a cigarette glow where Terry was leaning next to the front door.

"He's not here?"

Terry shook his head.

"But we would have passed him on the road," I said.

"Well," Terry said, "he's got to come sooner or later."

As it turned out, it was just after daybreak when we heard the wagon.

Crossing the yard Max looked at us, but he kept

on heading the team for the barn. We walked toward him, approaching broadside, then Max turned the team straight on toward the barn door and we could see the wagon bed. Regalo wasn't in it.

Max stepped off the wagon and waited for us with his hands on his hips.

"He ain't here."

Terry asked him, "What happened?"

"He jumped off the wagon and I lost him in the dark."

"And you've been looking for him."

Max grinned that ugly grin of his. "Sure," he said. "A man don't like to lose his top hand."

Then, glancing at Terry, seeing a look on the boy's face I'd never witnessed before, I knew Max Repper was about to lose his top teeth.

Sure enough. Terry took two steps and a little shuffle dance and hit Max square in the mouth. Max went back, but didn't go down and now he came at Terry. Terry had his right cocked, waiting, and he started to throw it. Max put up his guard and Terry held the right, but his left came around wide and clobbered Max on the ear. Then the right followed through, straightening him up, and the left swung wide again and smacked solid against his cheekbone. Max didn't throw a punch. He wanted to at first, then he was kept too busy trying to cover up. I thought Terry's arms would drop off before Max caved in. Then, there it was, for a split second—Max's chin up like he was posing for a profile—and Terry found it with the best-timed, widest-swung roundhouse I've ever seen.

Max went down and he didn't move. Terry stepped inside the barn and came out with a hackamore. He looked down at Max and started to roll him over with his boot. But then he must have thought, What good will it do— He turned away, dropping the hackamore on top of Repper.

All Terry said was "Long as the boy got away . . . that's the main thing."

★ ★ ★

AFTER THAT EVERYTHING was quiet for a while. Of course what had happened made good conversation, and wherever you'd go somebody would be talking about the half-wild white boy who'd lived with Apaches. And they talked about Max Repper and Terry. Everybody agreed that was a fine thing Terry did, loosening Max's teeth . . . but Terry better watch himself, the way Max holds on to a grudge with both hands and both feet.

Terry went back to his diggings and Deelie wore her tragic look like he was off to the wars. Max would come in about once a week still, but now he didn't talk so much. Ordered what he wanted and got out.

Then one day a man named Jim Hughes came in and told how he'd seen the boy.

Jim had a one-loop outfit a few miles beyond Repper's place. I told him it was probably just a stray reservation buck, but he said no, he came through the willows to the creek off back of his place and there was the boy lying belly down at the side of the creek. The boy jumped up surprised not ten feet away from him, scrambled for his horse, and was gone. And Jim said the boy was wearing a red shirt, the back of it all ripped.

Max heard about it too. The next day he was in asking whether I'd seen the boy. He talked about it like he was just making conversation, but Max wasn't cut out to be an actor. He wanted to find that boy so bad, he could taste it, and it showed through soon as he started talking.

Within the next few days the boy was seen two more times. First by a neighbor of Jim Hughes's who lived this side of him, then a day later by a cavalry patrol out of Dos Fuegos. They gave chase, but the boy ran for high timber and got away. Both times the boy's red shirt was described.

Now there was something to talk about again; everybody speculating what the boy was up to. The cavalry station received orders from the commandant at Fort Huachuca to bring the boy in and be pretty damn quick about it. It didn't look good to have a boy running around who'd been stolen by the Indians. This was something for the authorities. Down at the State House Saloon they were betting five to one the cavalry would never find him, and they had some takers.

Most people figured the boy was out to get Max Repper and was sneaking around waiting for the right time.

I had the hunch the boy was looking for Terry McNeil. And when Terry finally came in again (it had been almost a month), I told him so.

He was surprised to hear the boy had been seen around here and said he couldn't figure it out. Thought the boy would be glad to get away.

"Why would he want to go back to Apaches?" I asked him.

"He lived with them," Terry said.

"That doesn't mean he liked them," I said. "I could see him going back to those Mexican people, but Sahuaripa's an awful long way off and probably he couldn't find his way back."

Terry shook his head. "But why would he be hanging around here?"

"I still say he's looking for you."

"What for?"

"Maybe he likes you."

Terry said, "That doesn't make sense."

"Maybe he likes red shirts."

"Well," Terry said, "I could look for him."

"It would be easier to let him find you," I said.

"If that's what he wants to do."

"Why don't you just sit here for a while," I suggested. "The boy knows you come here. If he wants you, then sooner or later he'll show up."

Terry thought about it, making a cigarette, then agreed finally that he wouldn't lose anything by staying.

Right in front of me Deelie threw her arms around his neck and kissed him about twelve times. I thought: If that's what having him around just a little while will do, what would happen if he agreed to stay on for life?

★　★　★

DURING THE NEXT four days nothing happened. There weren't even claims of seeing the boy. Terry said, well, the boy's probably a hundred miles away now. And I said, Either that or else he's closing in now and playing it more careful. Repper came in once and when he saw Terry he got suspicious and hung around a long time, though acting like Terry wasn't even there.

The night of the sixth day we were sitting out on the porch talking and smoking, like we'd been doing every evening, and I remember saying something about working up energy to go to bed, when Terry's hand touched my arm. He said, "Somebody's standing between those two buildings across the street."

I looked hard, but all I saw was the narrow deep shadow between the two adobes. And I was about to tell Terry he was mistaken when this figure appeared out of the shadows. He stood there for a minute close to one of the adobes, then started across the street, walking slowly.

He came to the steps and hesitated; but when Terry stood up and said, "Regalo," softly, the boy came up on the porch.

Deelie turned the lamp up as we went inside and I heard Terry asking the boy if he was hungry. The boy shook his head. Then we all just stood there not knowing what to say, trying not to stare at the boy. He was wearing the torn red shirt and looking at Terry like he had something to tell him but didn't know the right words.

Then he reached into his shirt, suddenly starting to talk in Spanish. He pulled something out wrapped in buckskin, still talking, and handed it to Terry. Then he stopped and just watched as Terry, looking embarrassed, unwrapped the little square of buckskin.

Terry looked at the boy and then at me, his eyes about to pop out of his head, and I saw what he was holding . . . a raw gold nugget.

It must have been the size of two shot glasses;

way, way bigger than any I'd ever had the pleasure of seeing. Terry put it on the counter, stepped back, and looked at it like he was beholding the palace of the king of China.

He just stared, and the boy started talking again in that rapid-fire Spanish like he was trying to say everything at once. Terry looked at the boy and he stared some more until the boy stopped talking.

"What'd he say?" I asked him.

Terry took a minute to look over at me. "He says this is mine and that he'll show me a lot more. A place nobody knows about . . ."

I could believe that. You don't find nuggets that size out in the road. And it made sense the boy might know of a mine. It was common talk that any Apache could be a rich man, the way he knew the country—the whereabouts of mines worked by the Spanish two and three hundred years ago. Sure Indians knew about them, but they weren't going to tell whites and be crowded off their land quicker than it was already happening. In three years with Chiricahuas, Regalo could have learned plenty.

I said, "Terrence, you and that red shirt have made a valuable friendship."

★ ★ ★

TERRY WAS STILL about three feet off the ground. He said then, "But he claims he wants to live with me!"

"Well, taking him in is the least you can do, considering—"

"But I can't—"

He stopped there. I turned around to see what Terry was looking at and there was Max Repper in the doorway, with his Henry. Max was grinning, which he hadn't done in a month, and he came forward keeping the barrel trained at Terry.

"I knew he'd show," Repper said, "soon as I saw you hanging around. I came for two things. Him"—he swung the barrel to indicate the boy—"and my nugget."

"Yours?" I said.

"The boy stole it from me."

"You never saw it before you peeked in that window."

"That's your say," Repper answered.

Terry said, "What do you want with the boy?"

"I got work for him till the reservation people take him away."

"He doesn't belong on a reservation," Terry said.

"That's not my worry." Repper shrugged. "That's what they're saying at Dos Fuegos will happen to him."

Terry shook his head slowly, saying, "That wouldn't be right."

Repper lifted the Henry a little higher. "Just hand me the nugget."

Terry hesitated. Then he said, "You come and take it."

"I can do that too," Repper said. He was concentrating on Terry and started to move toward him. His eyes went to the nugget momentarily, two seconds at best, and as they did the boy went for him. He was at Repper's throat in one lunge, dragging him down. Terry moved then, pushing the rifle barrel up and against Repper's face. Repper went down, the boy on top of him, and then a knife was in Regalo's hand.

Deelie screamed and Terry lifted the boy off of Repper, saying, "Wait a minute!" Then, in Spanish, he was talking more quietly, calming the boy.

Repper sat up with his hand to his face. He had a welt across his forehead where the rifle barrel hit, but he was more mad than hurt. He said, "You think I'm going to let you get away with this?"

Terry was himself again. He said, "I don't think you got a choice."

"I haven't?" Max said. "I'll make damn sure he gets put the hell on that reservation."

"If you can prove he's Indian," Terry answered.

Max gave us his sly look. "Either way," he said. "If he ain't Indian then he's white, with white kin, and no authority's going to let him get adopted by a saddle tramp who ain't worked in two years."

It was a good thing Max was sitting down when

he said that. Max was through, and he probably knew it, but if Terry wanted the boy, then he'd sure make it plain hell for Terry to keep him.

I told Repper, "That's up to the authorities. The thing is, this boy's got no recollection of white kin and the only other person who knew his parents is dead. And he's said himself he wants to live with Terry."

Max grinned. "And I imagine Terry wants the boy, and his nugget, to live with him. But like I said, the authorities won't see it that way."

And then Deelie had something to say. She was looking at Max Repper, but I think talking to Terry, and she said, "No, they wouldn't let the boy live with a saddle tramp who hasn't worked in two years . . . but I'm sure they would agree that a successful mining man of Mr. McNeil's character would be more than they could hope for . . . especially since he'll be married within the week."

That was exactly how Deelie did it. I've often wondered if she ever thought Terry married her just so he could raise the boy. I didn't think he did, knowing Terry, and I doubt if Deelie really cared . . . long as she had him.

The stories contained in this volume originally appeared in the following publications:

"Cavalry Boots," *Zane Grey's Western*, December 1952

"Under the Friar's Ledge," *Dime Western Magazine*, January 1953

"Three-Ten to Yuma," *Dime Western Magazine*, March 1953

"Long Night," *Zane Grey's Western*, May 1953

"The Captives," *Argosy*, February 1955

"Jugged," *Western Magazine*, December 1955

"The Kid," *Western Short Stories*, December 1956

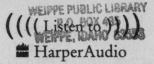